Twisted Tales from the Universe

Twisted Tales from the Universe

Star Lady Tales Book 2

Mari Collier

Published 2019 by Next Chapter
Cover art by Creative Paramita

Acknowledgement

Thanks to the members of the Desert Writers Guild and the Creative Writing Society for their critiques and encouragement.

Contents

One Flesh

The only viable industry left on Atlantis is a glorified auction block and I'm one of those up for bid.

Oh, there are still wealthy individuals here that can flit to the high places and afford the imported foods and clothes, but their servants are mostly robots. A lucky few real humans are employed as servants. There is nothing left on Atlantis but empty collapsing buildings, dust blowing in from destroyed land and foul tasting water from the few sources left.

"Next to stand is Nadja Dilum, a sturdy young female that should be able to bear your children without artificial procedures."

Someone behind me prodded my buttocks to make sure I walked briskly to the podium. The beautiful women had all been bid for and purchased, the action had been rapid. Most expected the pace of the bidding to slow and some men and women had left the hall. I am not one of the beautiful ones. I'm too tall, my eyes are too small, my shoulders too broad, my breasts are my own, and I have a straight up and down body with thick legs. It comes from growing up on the planet of Atlantis, the first one settled by pioneers from Earth. Earth beings in top physical condition had been a requisite for the colonists. My one good feature is a mane of thick, glossy black hair.

At one time Atlantis had been the richest planet in the galaxy. Ambitious males and females fled the planet as it waned. Anyone with half a credit or a degree still does. One of the resources Atlantis has left is an imbalance of females. To feed their extended families poorer women like me voluntarily offer themselves to an interplanetary bonding house. The bonding contract will pay a lump sum to the family on Atlantis and provide security in one's own old age. The bondage can be beneficial or lead to a shortened life full of misery. A few are extremely fortunate. They are showered with luxuries undreamed of by Atlantis's standards. Everyone one of us harbored a "what if it's me?" thought.

The bidding for me was not brisk, but two different males opened. After the fifth raise, the auctioneer banged the bell and announced, "Sold to Bitten VonMerg from Delmorph.

My brain had difficulty realizing that he was possibly as wealthy as the early bidders. He would be able to provide for my Mum and security for me. Delmorph is the financial powerhouse among the stars. My buyer was of medium male height which meant we saw eye to eye. His hair was dark as were his eyes, but his shoulder were round and it seemed his bodysuit revealed strange lumps patterned on his torso and thighs. Probably from sitting while arranging all those money deals, I thought. Well, so much for any chance of sexual satisfaction. The man would be more interested in financial accumulation.

Once he paid the auctioneer, he took my hand in his and said, "Welcome into my life." Hand in hand we walked to the outer chamber.

There the attendant handed me a soft green robe with a satin like sash and a pair of metallic green stretch shoes.

"I decided on a free flowing cover until we purchase your new clothes. It's rather inadequate, but it is serviceable. If you feel you wish to wear what you once owned, I'll understand." His voice was a decent tenor.

The feel of the material was incredible; soft, rich, supple beyond belief. Compared to the clothing I wore this morning, it was light years beyond in quality.

"Thank you, these are lovely." I quickly belted the robe around me, not that I'm overly modest you understand, but it was a tad cool in here. The shoes slipped onto my feet as though melded there and they were soft, oh so wondrously soft. I floated into the Bonding Chamber.

"Welcome Mr. VonMerg." The dark suited man at the desk looked like he was choking from the tightly rolled collar around his neck. He eyed my height with disdain. "I'm surprised. Your deposit entitled you to one of the first sold.

"This one suits my idea of a perfect body structure."

That took my breath away. My shoulders were as broad as his.

Signing the contracts took about one-half hour and rolled collar performed the brief allegiance ceremony. I learned Delmorphs tend to be old fashion. Bitt selected the wording from an ancient Earth wedding ceremony.

"The words 'until death do us part' need to be changed." Bitt insisted.

Instead of until death do us part, I found myself intoning, "We shall be one flesh."

Then we signed more papers. The amount to be paid to my mother was less than my purchase price, but I had the satisfaction of seeing my mother's worn face appear with tears streaming down her cheeks when she was informed of the amount deposited in her name.

"Will you regret leaving her, my dear?

"Yes and no, Mr. VonMerg."

"Please, address me as Bitt."

He did not wait for an answer, but took my hand and led me out to the waiting area. There he gave a triangular piece of metal or plastic to the attendant. Within minutes a fliver was at the station and we were whisked to his rooms high above the grey cloaked, broken city streets. The landing area was part of his suite.

"Here we are, my dear. What do you think of your new quarters?" He voice was full of anticipation.

I had to grab his arm for support. How do I describe carpets that are soft and glowing with colors? Would anyone believe me if I told them of four huge chairs, a long couch with a back, soft, glossy cushions, and rows of softly humming machines? There was a rich, deep brown table by the window with four maroon comfort chairs set around it. A beautiful center piece of flowers in a vase that looked like real glass, artwork from other planets emblazoned the walls with colors, and there were more rooms beyond this one.

"I believe I should order you some new clothes before we begin our celebration. What size do you wear?"

The question left me blank. I never knew clothes came in sizes. We always wore whatever we could find. If it was too large, belt it up, roll up the legs and waist, or cut them off if too long.

"I—I don't know."

"Hmm, very well." He brought a screen to life. "Coordinator, would you send up some female attire for someone, oh let's say about six feet tall, slender, unknown size. Is that possible?"

"For you, Mr. Von Merg, anything. Do you have any color preference?"

Bitt regarded me. "Oh, I should think any color but yellow will suffice. Tomorrow I'll expect a fashion courtier with a mini boutique, but not this evening. Also send up the dinner I ordered earlier, but for two." He blanked out the screen.

"See how easy that is, my dear. Let's do a tour of these rooms, and then you may freshen up and I'll contact a few places before dinner arrives. After that the evening is ours."

I had to be in a fantasy world. Unlike my former life, everything was plush. The bathroom is larger than my mother's allotted space, and everything is so clean.

Bitt showed me how to operate the buttons for the water and soap, where the lotions were, and left me alone. I took a very deep breath and cautiously stuck a foot into the sunken bath. The water was warm. Step by step I entered the water and lowered myself. Once there I closed my eyes and snapped them open. Everything was still there. This was not a fantasy. My body was wet, the sides of the tub real, the soap smelled heavenly, and everything was at my disposal.

When I finally walked back into the room, the dinner was there and Bitt was still at the screen, his face intent while his fingers touched the circles so rapidly they were blurring. He must have seen my reflection for he turned his head slightly, nodded, and spoke in a low tone.

"Clinch that price, Jarnel, and sell the instruments to the Decas."

He turned to me, "Lovely, my dear, you no longer smell of disinfectant. I didn't want to distress you, but it does have an odor."

Dinner was a revelation. One bite and I knew this was real meat, not the protein paste that was distributed twice a month at the feeding stations. There were real vegetables, the desert was real passion fruit with some type of syrup, and the wine must have been real too. There was no vinegary taste and I drank three glasses.

"That was wonderful," I said and giggled. What was wrong with me?

Bitt smiled. "The busser will be here to clear this away. Come." And he led me by the hand into the bedroom and closed the door. "We won't need to worry about interruptions."

Later I learned you call the servants by pressing a circle on the dinner tray. Well trained ones know exactly why and what to do.

He left the light on. "It adds to the pleasure, you know."

Well, no, I didn't, but why argue with someone that owns you?

He began by disrobing me, running his hands down my arms and sides. Then he began shedding his clothes. Delmorph clothing tends toward full sleeves, tight tubes around the body, and trousers that balloon below the knee. Bitt's clothes were a deep teal color. I didn't know whether to stand, sit, go full spread on the bed, or assume some other position. He'd been strangely silent on that point.

Bitt solved the problem by sitting on the bed and motioning me beside him. Then the lesson in Delmorph sexual practices began. It seemed all those strange bumps on his torso and thighs were to be stimulated. I must say he took his time to stimulate certain zones of my body. When it was over some two hours later darkness had dispelled grey sunlight, and I had experienced sheer ecstasy for the first time in my twenty-five or so years. I tingled in places I didn't know I had.

The next day courtiers, salon specialists, and tutors arrived. I was transformed into a classy, refined Delmorph. Everywhere I turned luxury abounded. Before we relocated to Delmorph, we spent two weeks touring places on my planet that I didn't know existed.

On Delmorph it was tutor after tutor. At last a different type of tutor appeared. "Now you learn about finances and whatever area it takes to make you a contributor to the VonMerg holdings." Bitt would disappear during the day as he caught up on financial work and changes. During the evening, he insisted we be together every moment.

"Why?"

"It is necessary for proper bonding."

Silly me, I thought we had. It was more than evenings that we spent together. Any free time we would visit other businesses, study together, shop together, and we always, always slept together whether we had sex or not. After five years of this regime, I felt it would be heaven to go shopping alone or find someone else to join me for lunch. I missed the intimate talk with friends of my own sex. I tried to take advantage of his mood after one particularly satisfying bout of sex. We had risen from the bed, but I was still tingling and we were both coated with a light film of sweat.

"Bitt, why don't we find divergent interests for an hour or so every day? It might enliven our other experiences."

"No, that cannot be."

"Aren't you tired of seeing me almost every waking hour of the day?"

"That doesn't enter into it, my dear. We must become one and all to each other."

"Is that why you haven't introduced me to your family?" I'd seen a man he called his brother on the vision screen, but never in person. He, like Bitt, only discussed finances. Neither did they look alike, except for the lumpy body.

"Didn't you notice that the ancient Earthen ceremony said it best? Leave your parents and cleave to one another. Man and woman shall become one flesh. My other mates appreciated this in the end."

"You've been bonded before?" How had I not known?

"Of course."

"You're separated?"

"Oh, no, my dear. Delmorphs live an incredible number of years by rejuvenating ourselves with contracts of allegiance. The extra time allows us as a family to grow and amass fortunes." This was puzzling as I had seen very few children.

"How many partners have you had?"

"Ten or twelve, I would need to recapitulate all their names."

"Were there any children?"

"No, there won't be unless I marry a Delmorph, but that is not likely. You may have noticed the Delmorph couples tend to age normally."

"Did all of your other bonders die of old age?" My contract strictly lined out my remuneration should separation occur or abandonment in old age.

"Not really, my dear, we became one flesh. They are all alive in me. Someday we will be one flesh. That is why you must learn every aspect of my business."

"How long does this take?" This conversation was beginning to make me uneasy.

"It varies, but anywhere from five to fifteen years." He smiled.

"Are you saying that when we merge into one flesh, we will truly be one as we vowed?"

He swept me into his arms. "You are so clever, my dear."

For the first time since we pledged allegiance, I fought to free myself. Merging didn't sound pleasant.

Bitt was stronger than I anticipated. He caught my arms and held them against my back and locked his mouth on mine. I tried twisting my body, but he put his thighs against the outside of my thighs and started squeezing. Those strange bumps that had been part of our sexual encounters latched onto my flesh like suckers, drawing me into his body mass and darkness descended. I wanted to scream, but my mouth wouldn't open and air wasn't coming into my lungs; yet I lived. I had sensations and they were wrong. I need air! I need to see! I need to live!

A voice seemed to speak in my mind. 'Don't fight me. We will be one: one Delmorph.

Another silent voice broke into his, 'envision bringing your arms across your chest and turn.

It took every ounce of my remaining strength and mind, but I managed to feel the sensation of my arms moving against flesh and vein while I twisted my body in a slow revolution.

Two voices in my senses were shouting, 'No.' One voice was mine and one was Bitt's.

That shadowy whisper seemed to grow in desperation. 'Now, thrust your arms outward.

I tried to achieve what was commanded. For a moment there was no sensation. Blackness and pain were blotting out my core—my sense of self. It felt like my scalp was being torn from my head.

No, my own being was screaming. I am alive. I need to see. I want to flex my fingers. I want texture. I want life!

My fingers tingled and moved. My eyes blinked and the room was a blurry mass. The other voice yelling 'No!' was retreating. My breath was ragged and I heard my voice, deeper as if I had a cold, but my voice saying, "I am alive. I am Nadja. I am I!"

I blinked again and there was the room. It looked the same. I looked downward at my body. My boobs had shrunk and those strange lumps were on me. Something was tickling my chest and I staggered into the bathroom feeling the need to vomit and that faint voice whispering, 'Cut it off., cut it off.

One look in the mirror stopped my stumbling steps. The tickling came from the mass hanging from my protruding lips and jaw line. It was my hair, gloriously glossy black, cascading down to my chest. It was mine. That Delmorph had not swallowed me whole. I was here physically.

The faint voice was chanting, 'Cut it off, shave it, be a true Delmorph.

Fat chance. That was me. Bitt couldn't have me. Not my core.

* * *

The beard remained. It does not matter how long I live or do not live. The balance in Bitt's account is enough to sustain me in luxury for nine Atlantis life spans. My black beard is truly luxuriant.

The Colony

Stark white moonlight created towering shadows as Cameo wandered among the stones serving as markers for the dead, but the music from the black, glistening compound where the Colony was celebrating their twenty-fifth year of operations floated through the winter air and mocked her. There was no one her age to dance with and she hated seeing her mother twirling merrily in some other man's arms.

She had fled the ComQuaCo compound for the night air. A dry, warm breeze was blowing from the west. Directions, however, meant little when there was nowhere else to go. ComQuaCo restricted all buildings and workers to the area for the mining and crating the crystals. Cameo did not belong here and there was no other place for her. When her mother birthed her almost sixteen years ago, there was no ship leaving.

When the freighter arrived with supplies and to pick up the ore containers, the captain refused passage. There was no one to care for a baby or facilities for one on board. It wasn't his fault some stupid woman had inhaled too much smooth, neglected her dosage, or forgot to use proper techniques. He would forward a request for permission for the baby to be relocated to an inhabited planet. The permission never came. Nothing in the mining camp provided for child care or schooling. There were no other children and very few women. Most of the women who were here were hard and rocky like the landscape of Diode. Her mother, Flow, was no different. Flow had shed no tears for her man partner of seventeen years when he died three days ago. Cameo found herself alone and completely friendless.

She had cried for two nights. Her father had told her stories when she was little and insisted she learn the symbols that made words and numbers. He was the one who explained to her how the black crystal roofing and outer walls drew the sun's energy into the spidery sheathing beneath it to be dispersed throughout the compound for power. He explained how the next layer of milk white, crushed crystals combined with insulating slur reflected any heat back into the sheathing. Now there was no one to teach her or smile in approval. The Colony required adults. When the body became too old to work the mines, they would be sent to an outpost set up for the aged. Good food and living quarters would be provided, but she didn't believe it as she knew of no one who had ever left the colony except by death. Neither did the other inhabitants, and they devised ways to create extra smooth for inhaling or snorting. "Smooth away all troubles for we die here," was the philosophy of the colony. Cameo hated and feared the mind-numbed smoothies that tried to grab her or any woman. She would break free, screaming as she ran from them. If the smoothies went too deep into their spaces, they died.

It wasn't until she had turned ten that her father told her that the laborers here were mostly low-level convicts and people adjudged incapable of learning the higher mathematics required for creating machines to do the work once done by humans or creating more efficient energy transformers. People sent here would eventually die from the crystallized dust of the planet.

Already the breeze was strong enough to make her bend her slight frame until she found the marker for her father's grave. Soon his grave would be difficult to find unless a larger stone was found to place above it. Sand had sifted into the ruts left by the earth digging machine and flowed over the lowest stones. His fellow workers had piled the rocks on as a tribute to a man that had been here almost from the beginning. The day after his death she had watched her mother don her father's working clothes.

"Hiton says I can have the job of inspecting for missed diamonds."

"The machines can do that. Those protective clothes didn't protect him from the dust. You'll die just like him."

Her mother shrugged. "Do you prefer starving? We can't leave here until we're old. It's time you started learning about the machines or how to please one of the miners. I'll do this until one of the important ones needs more personalized care."

Flow gave a final pat to her dark hair and sat to pull the helmed skel-suit on. She wiggled a bit and Cameo could see her frowning through the front plate.

"I need to exchange this for a tighter one. It isn't safe." Her voice had sounded muffled to Cameo's ears.

"You'd better have the meal ready when I get back. No more vis-uscreen games for you. No one here is going to pamper you anymore. The sooner you learn that, the sooner you'll make a good connection."

Cameo found herself sobbing again. She stumbled out of the grave area and tried to walk briskly. Sweat began forming on her forehead and body, her brown hair started to clump together from the sweat at her neck, but she went to the "field" area rather than return to the compound. It really wasn't a field, but one of the scientists who visited the Colony each year to inspect the crystal quality and designate where the machines and blasting minibots would chew into the planet's interior until the next turning had said the shocks of sandy, mustached lumps sitting there were the roots of dead plants. The wind had scoured the higher sand away. Sand dunes could be seen moving towards the dark, shadowy mountains. A dusty haze obscured any clear feature of the far off landscape. To Cameo, these were not roots, but wise, old creatures from some forgotten time. All you had to do was look at them and see the resemblance to mankind.

Winds had gouged features into the root balls. Grizzled, twiggy hair and mustaches covered most mouth areas. Smaller stems covered the partially opened eyes giving them the air of someone deep in thought. She went to the one she called grandfather. He looked so wise and the expression on his face was always compassionate as though he felt her sorrow and loneliness. The argument that a dead plant was devoid of emotion had no meaning to her. This was the kindest, wisest creature left in her world. Cameo threw her arms around his thick neck.

"Oh, Grandfather, I hurt so much inside. My father is dead and no one here loves me or cares about me."

Her tears trickled down into the dirt and twig collar ringing his neck. She felt the wind buffet them so hard that Grandfather shook.

"No, no, Grandfather, don't blow away. I couldn't stand it."

The lump of twiggy roots steadied and something edged into her mind like a soft brush writing words of reassurance.

There's no danger of being blown away. The moisture stirred me.

Cameo drew her breath in sharply and pulled away far enough to look up. It seemed as though the small, slender stems over his eyes had slip upward and far back in his head black coals gleamed.

"How can you give your thoughts to me? Dr. Pavel said you were a dead plant. Of course, I didn't believe him," she added. "I know you're real, Grandfather." She hugged tighter. It was as though he was comforting her, consoling her.

She stood upright as the blowing sand began scraping her skin and patted his mustache. "I'll come again, Grandfather, and bring you some real water."

Slowly she walked back to the compound. It would be difficult, but a few drops wouldn't be noticed.

Cameo spent the cooler mornings outside for no one could withstand the sun during the afternoon. She loved the brilliant blue sky, the unbroken, sandy landscape where plants had not grown in thousands of years. She began taking one-half of her daily drinking water ration with her and sprinkling a few drops on Grandfather. Sometimes it felt like she heard thank you or a low musical hum. Occasionally, she would be directed by the brushing in her mind to give the drops to a different member of the group. It was easy to imagine that Grandfather was growing stronger for underneath the golden beige twigs a fine, lighter beige color was slowly spreading. He seemed to favor extra drops going to the lump behind him and she would wonder why.

The features on that stump were less distinct and the twigs seemed to flow down the back. Perhaps a nose and eyes were there, but Cameo wasn't certain.

On her birthday, Cameo urinated beside him. Outside voiding was strictly prohibited as all wastes were measured and recycled. It seemed her only way to repay Grandfather's kindness. His broad front was the only contact with another creature she knew. Tomorrow she was to report to ComQuaCo's mine manager, Morph, for her assignment. She was certain it would be something she hated.

Morph grinned at her as she walked in. He was old, at least sixty. His skin was wrinkled and flecked with imbedded glints. Cameo didn't know if it was from the mines or if he had been one of the dreaded glazed ones the others whispered about. There was no hair on his head and his brown eyes appeared to be sunk in his head.

"Well, well, ready to take your place in production or would you rather warm my bed?" His silver streaked yellow teeth gleamed at her, but his eyes weren't smiling. They looked greedy.

"I'll work in the mines like everyone else." Cameo felt her insides shrivel. There had to be more to life than this old man.

His smile grew less brilliant, but his eyes gleamed. "Oh, you'll work all right. Work until I snap my fingers for you. Then you'll thank me."

Morph tossed a helmed skelsuit at her. "If needed, they'll issue the oxygen at the mine. Report to Hiton, now!" He watched her with those avid, devouring eyes as she went out the door.

The work was in the lowest sector, the area for making and placing the minibot explosives. Since she was the novice, it was her job to pack the plastics into the minibots. She missed her morning walks and real air. Her mother showed no sympathy for her, for Flow was living with another miner. Cameo was alone. Morph would not assign anyone to share her rooms. Always his eyes watched her.

After three months, Cameo was promoted to learning to drive the autocarts loaded with the minibots. She had been in the mines for almost six months when everyone was called topside shortly before quitting time. Another turning had passed, and the supply ship had sent a message.

Morph surveyed the group. "Listen up, miners. ComQuaCo will be here tomorrow. We'll suspend work for a day. Use it to clean up your sties and toss anything you won't need. Most of you long timers recognize that the quality and quantity of the crystals have diminished. It's reached the point it's no longer profitable. We'll be moving to where they designate. All petitions for formal recognition of contracts will be submitted to them. Flow has already signed over her girl brat to me."

He leered at Cameo before continuing.

"Any of you that want to change your arrangements have 'em in my section by 9:00 o'clock tomorrow. Any grievances should be there too." He glared at all of them; daring any of them to risk his retaliation. "Okay, earthgrunts, the rest of the day is yours. Rest well."

He strolled over to Cameo and grasped her arm. She'd tried to edge away, but her group had come up last and they were ranged against the wall.

"You can save a lot of problems if you come with me now. That way it will be a mutual agreement. The other way, you become dependent on me until they rule you can live independently."

Cameo stared at him in horror. "No, not this evening. I must talk with my mother first." She yanked her arm free and fled.

"How could you, Mother?" Cameo stormed as she caught up with Flow and Dan at the entry to their rooms. "He's ancient."

Flow had just opened the door, but she whirled on her daughter. "He's also the most important man on base. His apartment has four rooms, not two dinky ones like the rest of us." She held up her hand with thumb bent down and fingers in the air. "Count them: one, two, three, and four. He wants you; not me or one of the others that have been here for years."

"How do you know how many rooms he has?" Cameo's voice became a hoarse whisper. She looked from her mother to Dan, but he didn't care. He was smirking at her just like Morph.

"Oh, that was years ago." Flow waved her hand in the air dismissing infidelity as nothing. "How do you think we ate so well and had the extra electronics? They didn't appear because of your father. Just remember to 'ooh and aah' for him when you spread your legs. Now ex-cu-se us, we've things to do." The door slid shut behind them.

Shattered in heart and spirit, Cameo waited until evening and fled to Grandfather to wail out her woes. Once again her tears vanished into his twiggy face. This time it seemed as if his shoulders hunched. Somehow he came closer to her, and a soothing hum swept through her mind and body. Moonlight softened the world when Cameo returned to the huge structure that housed their quarters and the mine.

She awoke with swollen eyes and tried to eat, but the plate of food she'd withdrawn from the dinewell seemed to swell and lodge in her throat. She never liked the vile stuff they sent for the first meal. Lunches and dinners weren't too bad if you closed your eyes and smelled first, but the bland, grey early meal had no detectable odor. The protein drink that appeared with it smelled like fruit according to her father. He had lived on a real world with real food until he had been sent here. Her mother never spoke of where she was from. It was as though she never existed until she arrived here.

The visuscreen came to life as two ships descended for a landing. Music blared from the speaks and botcars pulled up to the ships. Three men and a woman alighted and took the enclosed botcar and headed for the compound. They were ComQuaCo's scientists and company rep. The most comfortable quarters would be theirs. No one inhabited those quarters during the months they were gone. Cameo thought it a big waste of space, but to speak such thoughts was dangerous.

Morph's face appeared speaking instructions. "You are to be at the assemblage in six hours. Anyone not there will be docked a turn's wages." Silence filled the room.

What difference could losing your wages make? Cameo was perplexed. Where would anyone spend their wages? There were no shops or places of entertainment like her father described. You took what was provided. Her mother bought extra electronics and food so perhaps there was a shop of some sort.

The assemblage was as boring as Cameo expected. The two scientists and technician were introduced, but the company female just sat surveying them all with a contemptuous sneer. Dr. Raugin spoke briefly. He stood before them, a slender man with smooth face, sallow skin, brown eyes, and dark, straight hair. He appeared to be about forty-five, but he could have been one hundred twenty-five for all Cameo knew of people from other parts of the galaxy.

"As you have been made aware, we will be moving these operations to a more productive area. It may be necessary to relocate your structure. The water will be off for approximately twelve hours if we do. You will be given ample warning and containers to store your water. We have three places in mind. Until a decision is reached, you will begin bringing the minibots up from below. Tomorrow you will report for your assignments as usual. Outside activity will be allowed. You'll be issued containers to begin packing your personal items. Anyone with contracts or grievances will meet with Cor Delay tomorrow at the main office. Be there at ten in the morning. You may pick up your personal crate as you leave—now."

As instructed everyone rose and filed from the room. Each picked up a crate and returned to their quarters.

Cameo looked at her rooms with a reverence few showed. It had been her home. Her mother had taken some of the items with her, but the visuscreen with its lessons and programs was built into the wall. She could not remove it. Cameo possessed few suits of clothing. What did it matter? They were all one piece and all a light green. Some of the women managed to bring scarves, but they wore out or blew away. She decided to leave her utensils in the drawer. No sense packing them as long as it was still three days away. She added a picture she had drawn for her father and then sat at the visuscreen. There was nothing else to do but watch it or play a math game. And how could she get away from Morph? The company rep wouldn't rule until tomorrow. Would a female ComQuaCo be more compassionate than her mother? The cold, pale female she saw on stage looked as though she hated everyone.

Cameo reported to work as usual, but the foreman sent her to the office at nine fifteen.

"You should clean up. ComQuaCo doesn't like slovenly workers."

Cameo considered. She felt as gray and gloomy as these walls, but maybe if she were clean the woman would see the despair in Cameo's eyes and realize she was too young to be joined to Morph. It would do her no good to hide in the fields. Their scanners would find her immediately.

Dutifully presentable, Cameo was at the office at ten a.m. A scowling Morph exited the office and glared at her. Had she been given a reprieve? She entered the office and looked at the ComQuaCo official. She could see nothing but dislike written on the woman's face and in her eyes.

"Don't bother sitting. You have been chosen to attend to Dr. Raugin." Her face was bitter, the mouth almost a snarl. "For some reason he prefers a more youthful companion while here."

The woman's eyes bored into hers. "I believe you're clever enough to know which apartments belong to us. Be there when he returns this evening, and remember, you must comply with his every wish or you will never leave this Colony even in old age. For now, you will return to work below. You'll have ample time to clean up after your shift. He just insists you be clean. He really won't care what you wear, if anything." The woman sniffed.

"Now go, the stench of you is more than I can bear."

Cameo stared at her momentarily and left without speaking. At least she wouldn't be contracted to Morph. But how was going to Dr. Raugin any better? She was quite aware of what every wish meant. The Colony's rooms were small and privacy was unknown. At an early age, she had seen and heard all that passed between her parents. She had another hour before reporting below and she fled outside into the dry, heated air that did not reek of other humans.

She ran swiftly to the field and threw her arms around Grandfather. "Oh, how I wish you were alive. Being contracted to Morph was horror, but now it's worse. I have to please Dr. Raugin, and I've never been with anybody. They are going to find another place to dig. They'll never let me off this planet." She hugged tighter. "No one cares about me here and no one will help me, Grandfather. You've gotten stronger, but you can't help me either."

It was true. Grandfather was no longer brittle. His twiggy hair and mustache had softened, and the dry, yellowish outer coat seemed sleeker, less rough. His shoulders were higher than hers. The other root balls with faces had straightened and she was sure they too were taller.

The warm tickling in her mind began again and her head was filled with the thoughts of water; lots and lots of water running over the field and soaking down, down, loosening the earth. Cameo shivered with the thought of how much better this part of her world would be if all the roots were alive again.

Water, all it takes is water.

The words brushed her mind, and she looked at Grandfather with widened eyes.

"I can't carry that much water to you. There's nothing to bring it in."

But the water is there. We can smell it. The voice grew stronger, more demanding. *Give it to us. We will do the rest. Else they will destroy us. There are life-giving minerals below us. You must bring the water to us. Then we will save you.*

Cameo gasped at the thought. The water was stored in a huge tank filling the center of the facility. All the apartments, labs, and offices circled it. Cameo knew the tank rose from the lowest mine shaft. The various tunnels for mining radiated into the surrounding rock. Below the ground level, workers would scurry around the huge tank to follow whatever instructions the office sent. After work, miners would stroll around the huge tower on the upper floors. It was their assurance that they would survive here in comfort. Few people ventured outside.

The metal tank was visible from every angle inside. The moment you stepped into the facility, you saw it. She would need to blow a hole in it, near the floor level for the water to run out and down towards the field where Grandfather rooted. To do that she would need to bring at least one or two minibots from below. How could she conceal them? If she were pleasing Dr. Raugin, she wouldn't be working in the mines. If she didn't do it, Grandfather might die and she would be friendless again.

She leaned against Grandfather and she felt his strength flowing through her veins. Somehow she would free her Grandfather, and he would rescue her. After one last hug she ran back to the facility.

Cameo was breathless and sweating as she boarded the last cage going down. The others must have heard of her new status as they drew away from her. Conversation ceased. They feared she would report something to Dr. Raugin, and they would suffer.

At the bottom, their foreman waited. He motioned for them to join the others waiting beside the door where supplies were stored.

"Listen up, diggers. Prelim sampling will be done tomorrow. Our eminent visitors have decided they will drill in the field and in the mountain area. Frankly, my belief is the field will win. ComQuaCo won't need to transport this facility or build another one for years. The prelims show a smaller facility by the field, but it won't be much. We'll just tunnel to it. First they need minibots with charges to start the drilling. We'll be taking them upside and stacking them by the field. If they roll off overnight and explode, it will just save having to blow out the root balls. Okay, line up by seniority, and we'll start ferrying them up. Each one will take an autocart and load it with two charged minibots. Then drive them to the fields. You'll be shown where to place them. Then return here for another load, if needed. The good news is our rooms may not be scheduled for destruction. All right, work time. Line up."

As the newest worker, Cameo stood waiting patiently. She was in a mining area filled with the people she'd known all her life; and she was alone.

She brightened as Flow walked up.

"What's the matter with you? You look like you are going to be sick. Go see the Meds if you aren't well. Dr. Raugin didn't come here to be contaminated."

"Please, Mum, how do I get out of this."

"Well, I certainly didn't raise anyone with brains. You don't want out of it. You want to dig it for all it's worth. You should be up at the office demanding the sweet smelling soaps and sprays that you need to prepare yourself for tonight." She glared at Cameo as Cameo shook her head and tears appeared in her eyes.

"You'll probably make an idiot of yourself. Have sense enough not to scream." She turned her back and walked forward.

The woman in front of Cameo turned. Like all of those that had been here for years, her face was wrinkled as though the dry air sucked every ounce of fluid from beneath the skin.

"Don't pay any attention to Flow. She's just mad that she is no longer young with smooth skin. She used to flaunt all the extra electrons she earned."

The woman's eyes saddened. "Poor baby, you've never had anyone your own age. Make sure he gifts you with something really good."

Cameo was almost crying. "I don't want to go to him."

Annoyance ran across the woman's face. "Don't be silly. You're the only young, unwrinkled one here. Use it for what it's worth." She turned her back.

Cameo was alone and isolated. Grandfather was the only one on her side, and he needed water. She looked at the towering water tank again. The metal couldn't be any sturdier than the stone the minibots blasted. If she could head towards the outside like everyone else, she could turn her autocart and drive straight to the tank firing her charges instead of placing them where directed. If she blew a large enough hole into the tank, the water would flow out the door and down the hill to Grandfather.

As Cameo drove her autocart towards the door, she noticed the first of the autocarts were returning. The older miner motioned for her to stay back. She smiled happily and whipped her autocart around and sent it hurdling towards the tank. At two feet from the tank she fired the charges and threw the autocart into reverse planning to put as much distance as possible between her and the explosion. People were yelling at her when the minibots exploded.

The huge tower split upward, water gushing out with tremendous force and speed. It spewed outward while the force of the surging water pulled more water upward and downward. Her autocart and the others were swept out the door. Caught in the roiling waters the mass poured down towards the field; closer and closer to Grandfather and the piles of roots. Dr. Raugin and his colleagues were caught as they tried to exit the field and were tumbled into the dunes.

The people in ComQuaCo.'s compound first floor offices watched in horror as water rose and whirled around their ankles and marched upward towards their knees. People folded, screamed, and died as the visuscreens started shorting out. The air supply ran by below ground equipment remained steady. Slowly the water level crept downward, and what few people were left staggered out to access their loss.

Morph was cursing at the airships lifting into the air.

"We're stranded. Look at those bastards run. They're not coming back." Suddenly, it occurred to him that whoever controlled the food might live long enough for another expedition to return. He fled to the lower region's warehouse.

Others gradually recovered and tried to care for the injured. Later, they bedded down for the night too frightened about their future to post any guards in this unpopulated, desolate area.

In the fields the water seeped down, down, down, seeking its ancient bed. The dry plants softened, then stiffened and straightened; the largest of them flexing arms that moved away from the sides, then standing, helping the next one and pointing to the far mountains.

"We need to recover our strength. The little one told me there are rivers there."

More and more ill formed twig people arose and shed their outer coating of dust and debris. They waded behind the largest form. In the middle of the field-lake, Ashen stooped and picked up a slight form. Hurriedly, she carried it to Billow. Billow would wish to see the stranger before they disposed of her and her kind.

"Does she still live?

"No, she has grown cold."

"We will take her with us."

"Why not leave her?"

"She saved us. We can rebuild again. When we reach a safe place, we will encase her in the life giving clay of this world as a reminder that one human helped us to revive. Her features will remain and her hands outstretched to deliver water. We'll take some of the others of her type with us. They'll be placed around her as attendants. She is an example of extreme love and sacrifice. Our earth has nutrients. Who knows, maybe even enough for aliens."

Centuries passed as the housing and industries flourished. Centuries later, the bright lights and machines fled outward and then returned to a darkened planet to be used as a mining colony.

A girl with coarse, beige hair wandered out to the ruins area called Billow after the mythical founder of their race. Of course, everyone denied that Billow was an actual, living man; nor did he ever have a consort named Ashen. They agreed that the ancient ones on this planet created the technology that allowed her race to access the galaxies. Now the planet had degenerated into a desolate area; fit only for a colony of miners extracting the life giving sands and clay to be shipped to the populated areas of other worlds. She stopped in front of a standing, yet slumping figure with outreaching arms to welcome her. It mattered little to Mahan that the others laughed at her. To her it looked like a lumpy, grandmother stretching out her arms to give comfort. The sorrow in Mahan's heart overwhelmed her and she threw her arms around the beige, stick encrusted rock.

"Oh, grandmother, my world has ended." Her tears cascaded down unto the surface of the beige lump. Comfort and warmth seemed to flow from the figure, easing Mahan's sadness and Mahan hugged tighter. She seemed to hear a thank you for the balm of water pass through her mind like a gentle brush and she felt her pain ease.

A Visit From The Tooth Fairy

Wilbur bit down on the BLT, the smoky, apple flavor of the bacon washed over his palette and his molar snapped. He ran his tongue over the jagged edge and extracted the broken snag from his mouth.

He glanced around the crowded lunch group at the Twentynine Palms Inn, but everyone at his table was too busy talking about the latest removal of the City Manager without any reason. The other people packed into the small space were either toney tourists or locals meeting for lunch to be seen or to look at the new artwork hanging on the walls. Wilbur slipped the tooth into his shirt pocket behind the eyeglass case. Maybe his dentist would want to see it.

He called his dentist as soon as he was back in his office. "Does it hurt," was the question that greeted his request for an appointment.

"No, but I'm apt to slice my tongue on it. The damn thing is sharp."

"Are you able to eat?" Was the next query.

Wilbur felt the ire raising, but tried to keep his voice calm. That was Cindy on the other end of the line, and she was a cute little thing. "Yes, of course, I finished my lunch with no problem."

"Well, come in tomorrow about one fifteen p.m. and Dr. Stanley will have a quick look at it. I'll also set you up for our next available appointment for a filling or a crown. That will be next month on the twenty-first; a Wednesday. Is that all right?"

By this time Wilbur was staring at the telephone in disbelief. He had not needed dental work before. He simply went in every six months for a cleaning.

"Why does it take so long for an appointment to do anything?" He was almost spluttering. "I could starve to death if something were really wrong."

"I'm sorry, Mr. Bilby, but we really are that busy, and you said you could eat and that there wasn't any pain. Is that incorrect?"

"No, I can eat, but it seems like a prolonged time."

"Yes, sir, will you be in tomorrow," she asked in her most professional voice.

"Of course, I'll see you then." He gritted his teeth as he said those words. He knew he could argue them into changing their minds when he saw them face to face.

* * *

Wilbur was still out of sorts when he went to bed that evening. He crumbled up his shirt and tossed it into the laundry hamper, but sleep came easily when he closed his eyes.

It was the movement of the pillow that awakened him, and he reached up and grabbed a hand.

"Let go of me," demanded someone.

Wilbur didn't let go for the hand was soft and smooth and the voice very feminine. He did a bolt upright.

"Who the hell are you?" he said and reached for the light with his other hand.

"No, don't turn on the light. You aren't supposed to see me. Where is the little boy that lost his tooth?"

Wilbur ignored her words and snapped on the light. He found himself looking a voluptuous, young woman in a white formal gown. Her hair was as white as her gown and her face and hand almost as white, except for the red, red lips. Her face is like an albino, thought Wilbur, and swallowed when he saw her eyes of lightest blue.

"This is all wrong. Why are you sleeping where the little boy is supposed to be sleeping and where is his tooth? I can't leave any money if I cannot bring his tooth back."

"There isn't any little boy, and I haven't lost a tooth. Just part of it snapped off, and why the hell are you pretending to be the Tooth Fairy. Did you think robbing me was so easy?"

"I have no idea what you are talking about. Where is the boy?"

"There's no kid here!" Wilbur was yelling. "I'm not even married."

"Oh, my, this is a bureaucratic screw up. Do you still have your tooth? I can take that back with me and prove that Millicent totally incompetent."

Wilbur was now fully awake and realized this was bizarre, but he wasn't buying the Tooth Fairy thing. The woman, however, was gorgeous, and he kept a firm grip on her hand.

"Look, lady, I don't know why you wandered in here, but we're both wide awake now. Let's forget about some old tooth, and have a drink. I've got some good Pinot Noir in the wine cooler. Then we can discuss what happens next."

She was looking at him in horror. "Sir, I need that tooth."

"You're not getting it until I know why you want it."

"Oh, very well, here's the dollar." Somehow a crisp one dollar bill had appeared in her other hand. "Now give me the tooth and we can exchange these items."

Wilbur snorted. "You just woke me out of a sound sleep. A dollar doesn't buy anything. Since you're giving away money, I'll take five hundred of those bills that just appeared in your hand"

Her lips drew together in a straight line. "I have other deliveries this evening. I cannot give you that amount for one tooth."

"It's just part of a tooth, remember? Let's start over. Maybe we can be friends." He smiled at her.

Wilbur had his second shock of the evening as she grew fainter and evaporated from sight. He was left blinking and staring at the wall. He ran a hand through his hair and shook his head.

That was the weirdest dream he had ever had.

"Why did I turn on the light?" He snapped off the light and returned to his pillow, still puzzled about his vivid dream. He hadn't thought of the Tooth Fairy in years. Why would he dream of her now? He had just broken off part of the tooth, not the whole thing.

The next day wasn't any better for Wilbur. The dentist was adamant that he needed a crown. The whole procedure was going to cost one thousand dollars. He could come in for a temporary crown tomorrow and have the crown affixed at the next month's appointment. Wilbur ground his teeth, but didn't curse at the girls. There went part of his down payment on a new T-Bird.

Wilbur also did some checking on dental prices and was amazed to discover that his dentist was charging the going rate. Big dental firms in places like Rancho Mirage or Palm Desert were charging even more.

That night he was awakened by someone shaking his shoulder.

"Do you still have that tooth? The office is being quite spiteful about the whole incident. They claim they can't be wrong! There are others waiting to take my place."

Wilbur looked up to see an angry face-flushed a delicate pink, Tooth Fairy.

"Why would I keep part of a tooth? I told you, I haven't lost a tooth, just part of it. Why don't you take a picture of my mouth and Instagram it?"

"What are you talking about?"

"Use your cell phone and send them a picture. That way I might get some sleep."

"We don't have such things in our world. There isn't any need. We can be any place and look at the other if it is really necessary, but why one would want to do so?

Wilbur woke up enough to remember he had slipped that broken part into his shirt pocket. It was in the laundry, and he was facing a thousand dollar dental bill.

"Forget spending the night with me. Just hand over one thousand of those dollar bills and I'll find the tooth."

"I will not. These dollars are for all of the little boys and girls who are relying on me." She took a deep breath. "Are you going to give me the tooth? I'll give you this dollar."

Once again the dollar appeared in her hand.

"As soon as you give me what I want, I'll give you the half-tooth. If you don't quit waking me in the middle of the night, I'll be asking for more."

The last was said to wall again. "Damn, how does she do that?"

Wilbur was beginning to feel the effect of being awaken every night, but he felt she wouldn't return after that last request. He went into a deep, sound sleep.

The next night he was awaken by the sounds of doors being opened and drawers pulled out and closed.

He snapped on the light and saw everything from his dresser and armoire dumped on the floor. He could hear another door opening and something crashing in the kitchen. He grabbed the valet tree and charged into the kitchen.

The Tooth Fairy twirled, the frying pan in her hand. On the floor were his utensils and various pots. "You are supposed to be asleep," she said.

"Hell, woman, who could sleep through that noise? Do you realize how long it will take to put all this back?"

"Give me the tooth and it will be done in an instant. See." She waved her hand at the silverware drawer to demonstrate. The silverware skittered across the floor in all directions and the drawer remained overturned on the floor.

Tears began flowing down her face. "See what you've done." She yelled at him. "They've taken my magic." Her face became whiter and her facial skin began to wrinkle. "Now there won't be a Tooth Fairy for all the little boys and girls. You are a monster!"

She disappeared.

Wilbur picked up all the silverware and utensils and staggered back to bed. He'd worry about putting them in the drawers and putting the clothes away tomorrow.

He stumbled out in the morning thankful for the automatic coffee brewer and grabbed a breakfast bar. Some of the utensils and silverware went into the drawers but not all.

The mess in the kitchen and the clothing on the floor told him that whatever was happening was not a dream. He was either sleepwalking while dreaming at night or acting out some deep-buried psychological problem. If the latter were true, then he had single-handily destroyed the Tooth Fairy. There was no way to prove that the Tooth Fairy no longer existed. It wasn't like the TV news would be broadcasting about a Tooth Fairy. Wilbur was perplexed and he wanted rid of his nightly visitor.

The news had nothing about a Tooth Fairy body or her death, and the children remained disruptive brats, but they weren't crying about a Tooth Fairy either. He considered calling the police to keep that woman out of his house. Then the thought of explaining the situation ended that notion. It looked like handing her the broken off part of the tooth was the only way to get rid of her. He dug in the laundry and pulled up the shirt. There in the pocket was the partial tooth. He stowed the tooth in the nightstand drawer beside his bed and began putting away all the socks and underwear that now resided on his floor. When he finished, it was eleven p.m. His kitchen once more had hidden, unused utensils and his clothes were more or less all neatly folded and stacked or hung back in the closet. He poured a glass of wine.

"Here's to you, Tooth Fairy, wherever you are." He lifted the glass high before taking a swallow.

"I'm right here. I have one more chance. Where is that tooth?" The voice came from behind him.

Wilbur spewed red wine over himself and the floor.

"Dammit women, don't scare me like that." He turned and saw a really old creature in a ragged white gown. Her hair was still white, but thinner and seemed to straggle downward as though the effort of growing was too much.

"What happened to you?"

"I told you. I need the tooth."

Wilbur set the glass down. "Give me a minute." He headed for his bedroom.

This dream became crazier and crazier and he had not even crawled into bed yet. He yanked out the drawer and removed the tooth.

"I looked there last night."

"It wasn't there last night." He handed her the tooth. It looked like the only way he was going to get any sleep.

"This is just part of a tooth."

"That's what I told you the first night. I just lost part of the tooth. It is going to cost a thousand dollars to have a crown to replace it. If the dentist did a root canal and implant it would be closer to five thousand."

She didn't bother to answer, but did her disappearing act again.

"Well, she could have at least thanked me," Wilbur grumbled. "But now maybe I can get some sleep."

Wilbur couldn't believe how well he felt the next day just from sleeping through the night. He really looked forward to the evening when he could pick up a pizza, watch his favorite show, and retire without worry. That night, he still set the alarm as a precaution to oversleeping.

He was awakened by a hand lifting his pillow. He grabbed at the hand, flipped on the light, and looked at the restored to her youthful, voluptuous figure, the Tooth Fairy.

"Now what? I gave you the damn tooth."

"Yes, but I forgot to give you the dollar in my rush to prove that Millicent is an incompetent hag."

"I don't want a damn dollar. All I want is a full night's sleep. That is, unless you've changed your mind and would like a glass of Pinot Noir."

"Don't be silly. I've umpteen deliveries to make this evening. Princess Adie is ever so much more efficient in blocking out the route." She bent and kissed his cheek.

Wilbur tried to embrace her, but she was gone.

He reached under the pillow to retrieve the dollar and his hand closed around a thick packet of bills wrapped with a yellow band stamped $1,000.00.

Elfor

We stood there in the chill of November, huddled against the cruel, gray air that whipped our coats and scarves, heads bowed as the Pastor said the final prayers for the grieving family and friends of Anna Swenson. When it was over, Tanya's son, Tylwyth, and I supported her back to the waiting rental automobile.

It wasn't devastating grief for her adopted mother's passing that immobilized Tanya. It was those idiotic high heeled, shoes she'd insisted on wearing to the cemetery. Now I, Elvie (short for Elvira) Fedderman, wore a sturdy pair of walking shoes. Southwestern Iowa terrain is noted for its treachery when coated with ice. The sky looked none too promising with billowing grey and black shaded clouds.

"Elvie, this is goodbye."

"But, the reception at your mother's house. They'll expect you."

"No, Tylwyth and I are leaving for Omaha immediately. We don't wish to be stranded here in a blizzard." She shrugged her slender shoulders. "So you see, Elvie, this is truly goodbye unless you take me up on the offer of free room and board in Seattle."

I was speechless for a moment while protests flickered in and out of the curves of my mind. It was true, they could be stranded, and Tylwyth's resemblance to Tom Pyke did him no favors. Some remembered. Already the mutterings had started; stifled to low, guttural whispers in respect for the Swenson family.

They were less severe on Tanya. She had spent the last three days with Anna. She never stirred from the room except for personal needs, and held Anna's hand while soothing her. Tanya did leave the room when Pastor arrived to give the Lord's Supper. She wasn't there for the benediction and the words "Peace be unto you." She did not see Anna's wrinkled face smooth into a smile and the restless turning and moaning cease. Tanya returned to the room when Pastor left.

But family and friends remember that Tanya shrugged off their words of Anna's last testimony, and their mood could grow ugly. They drew away from this blond, slender sprite that had been dumped in our farming community.

I glanced around and saw that my sister and husband had safely deposited Mama in their car and were waiting for me.

"Elfor," I lapsed into her old family nickname, "I can't. Who would take care of Mama?

"You could let Minnie do that for a month or two," she answered with asperity. "You need to visit a place where you can actually meet people that exist without bovine stupidities."

That was cruel. These people are my family and friends. I had always defended her. Granted, it grew more difficult each year. She openly proclaimed that she was a Wicca adherent, opened an occult store called Yarthkins, a truly outlandish name.

"But, Elvie," she protested when I suggested a name like Candlesticks, "it means Quiet Folk. That's what we are: quiet folk."

"Why not just join the Quakers?"

"It's not the same," she laughed, her strangely unwrinkled skin dimpling with amusement.

The cars were leaving, and the people behind us were becoming anxious. They wanted to put in an appearance at the reception and be safely at home before the storm hit.

Tylwyth lit a cigarette and scowled at his mother. "Let's get out of here,"

"We've changed too much, Elfor." We both knew my words were false, for we had not changed. "We would only quarrel."

She looked at me, her blue eyes hardening, and so did her skin underneath all that goo. "Elvie, why don't you admit that it was Pastor's superior strength that stopped us that Halloween Eve, and not the word of your so called God?" She slammed the door and the auto sped away before I could answer.

Deep in my own thoughts, I walked over to Minnie's car and got in. Elfor's belief in what had happened was the reason for my question to Pastor Hagendorf that long-ago night.

"Why did you have to hit him after using God's word?"

I was only seventeen and shaken by what I had seen. Who would believe chanting, naked bodies of both sexes dancing around a fire in Iowa in 1952? Oh, the world was changing. We knew that. What we didn't know was how fast it would change for all of us. My beloved Darrel Swenson, tall, broad, smiling, waving, his strong yellow teeth gleaming, had left Iowa. The army sent him to Korea. One year later, when they brought him back, there wasn't a funeral fixed smile on his face. His was a closed casket. I wept then, and I still weep for us today.

I drug my mind back to the present as I entered the car. I patted Mama's frail, trembling hand. After all, it was her friend of over seventy-five years we had buried today. I knew she wondered why she was left while all her vigorous friends and her own strong husband were gone. She needed comforting.

Later the memories that had lain dormant and buried in their own grave stirred and rushed back. To refute Elfor's words, I dredged up every bitter event, every glittering moment with Darrell that I had locked away. Every memory and every experience when one is young becomes etched in vibrant color, recorded and ready for instantaneous recall. Then years pass and the memories become over woven with everyday clutter, never to arise in a world now a comfortable monochrome of pastels.

Perhaps someone like Elfor could not help creating questions in our part of the world: Pocahontas County, state of Iowa. I could give you the township name too, but few care about that nowadays. Her arrival is still talked about in whispers.

She was an elfin, blonde sprite of two or three, abandoned by some passing traveler. By the time Anna found her in Swenson's lane, she was half starved and whimpering like an animal.

Anna Swenson had taken the collie to go after some cows across the road, and the dog had stopped to nudge the body partially hidden in the dry, stunted weeds. Then the collie sat and howled, driven by some wild instinct to protect the young. Anna gathered the child in her strong arms and ran home, the cows forgotten. God knows they had six already, and the depression and dry years made money scant, but they willing kept her. They tried half-heartedly to find her kin.

Tom Nelson was sheriff of Austin, our county seat and tried to question the child, deriving no more information than her name was Tanya. How on earth would anyone be able to get information from a child that young? Tom scratched his graying head and gave up. This was more frustrating than throwing some drunk in jail on a Saturday night and definitely required a different approach.

She could barely form words and would pronounce her name Tanya; the first syllable with a long a, the last syllable barely heard with a short a. She would giggle when the family called her Tanya with the short a in both syllables and stressing the last. The collie became her special guardian, even growling at the boys if they roughhoused too near.

Welfare was a lot different in those days. The county didn't have a place or money for an indigent child. They would need to send her to an orphanage and then pay for her upkeep. They gladly let the Swenson's take the responsibility. As Lars Swenson would say, "With six boys, this must be God's way of giving us a girl." Some sniffed at this bit of cornfield philosophy and wondered who and where she really came from.

But what did it matter? The blue-eyed sprite of joyful songs and laughter became Anna's special child. The year was 1937 and the depression was slowly loosening its grip on America and the world. The dry years had pushed people into migrations and violence rarely seen in this country. Europe was slowly spinning towards war. It was tragedy, but in those years children were abandoned by their defeated, jobless parents. The stubborn stock that farmed our section of the Midwest refused to budge. Somehow our parents found time to laugh even while their stock sickened and died; while crops withered in the fields; while cinch bugs and grasshoppers ate what little was left.

When the county granted the Swenson's custody of Tanya, they had her baptized at our Lutheran church. Her white gown was exquisitely tatted by Anna. My parents, Alfred and Bertha Fedderman were the sponsors as Lars and Anna had used all of their brothers and sisters on the boys. Tanya screamed while the Pastor poured the water and pronounced the words of the sacrament. Mamma and Anna used to laugh whenever they talked about it. Somehow the laughter was uneasy, as though neither would admit that some evil could lurk in such a small body or offer rebellion to the Lord's command.

Tanya and I were often together and we became fast friends. Our parents played pinochle of an evening when time and crops permitted. We attended the same church, the same one room schoolhouse (gone now–two acres growing corn instead of minds). I had no sister until I was fifteen when Mamma proved that though unspoken sex was not unknown. Those were good years to be young and alive with the world changing and new and exciting events. We knew the Lord was beside us and we could weather any kind of storm through family love and hard work. The outer world didn't really begin to intrude until 1949 when smooth roads and a small box with fuzzy pictures capable of expanding our wants began to change our mores.

I digress, but it is difficult to pick up the threads of life that must be sorted out or remained locked away. Maybe this way I can let Darrell go. He was two years older than Tanya and I; strong blond, maybe not handsome but rugged and filled with joy, touching a plant with tenderness, sifting the earth through his fingers. He was drafted during the Korean War. They called it a police action, but it was war that blew him apart. I cried with the Swenson's, but his death buried all of my memories of our time together and of my time waiting for him to return. It was but a few short months before his death that Tanya's father returned to our area.

The weekly newspaper didn't print anything about Tom Pyke's arrival in town. Nice simple name, isn't it? Not like the Nordic, Scandinavian, and German tongue twisters we were accustom to pronouncing. It wasn't just the name that set Tom Pyke apart. He was different. At first people tried to be fair. They blamed themselves for not liking him. He was skinny and slack of hip where we were stocky—healthy, if you please. His hair and skin blended into a mottled tan with no beginning or end. His brown eyes were almost red, and he'd wink slyly while making a point. Unfortunately, he didn't bathe. Not that anyone was too persnickety about daily bathing; once a week was sufficient for farm folk.

Tom Pyke bought the local junkyard, and goodness knows, junkmen weren't noted for cleanliness, but around him there floated an aura of something more, something worse than unwashed body dirt. It was as though his insides needed a good cleaning, and people began avoiding the yard, sometimes even taking their junk to another town. The young, however, found his place fascinating. They would arrive there to smoke and plot their night adventures as if to flaunt their daring to their peers by treading where their parents would not. Of course, I found out about it from Tanya.

"Come on, Elvie, it's fun. We talk about all sorts of things like old religions and different customs. I've even had something to drink."

"Really? What kind of pop?"

"Oh, silly, I mean a beer or some wine." She laughed. "Of course, he serves wine straight from the bottle or in a jelly glass. I think the bottle's cleaner."

"Why go there then? You've had that at home."

"Don't be silly. I can have only one beer the whole weekend and they only serve wine on a holiday."

"Then you're drinking more than one." It was a statement, not an accusation, but Tanya took it that way.

"Well aren't you the goody-goody." She flounced off to her next class.

At church that Sunday, we made up. Next Friday at school (we were seniors), Tanya had an invitation for me.

"I know you haven't gone anywhere without Darrell since he came back from boot camp, but after he leaves, why not come with me to roast marshmallows on Halloween? I don't have a date that night as I think trick or treating is so juvenile. We'll just be nice and cozy by a fire and figure out what we're going to do after graduation. Plus, I want you to look really close at Tom Pyke. I think he's my father and came here to find me. Okay?"

"Ah, sure." I sighed. "But, Elfor, I'll be horrible company." Just the thought of Darrell going to Korea made me sick inside; so sick that I forgot and called her by her family nickname at school. As a freshman, she had absolutely forbid it and had not relented one whit. For once she didn't appear upset.

"It's a date, Elvie, just us girls." She smiled and winked at me before heading to class.

That night while we sat in Darrell's car, I told him how Elfor and I had made up and who I would be with on Halloween. I mean, she was his little sister and he'd been upset when we had a falling out.

"As long as you only let the fire warm you and no one else." He pulled me closer. "I think Rudy is planning on being there too even though he is a little young to be driving."

"You drove at that age." In fact, all of us farm kids did. We were driving tractors before we were twelve and the clutch on a car wasn't nearly as heavy. Of course, the car was faster and there were a lot more gears to a car then the tractor, but that was then, not now.

"Gee, Darrell, Tanya sounded like it would just be us." And then I promptly forgot about it until after Darrell left.

That is, I forgot until I overheard Joe Davenport arguing with Leo Schaffer as they walked out of study hall.

"Ain't no way I'm going there on Halloween. Pyke's up to no good."

"How do you know, Joe?"

"Cause any junkman that can afford to serve that much liquor to kids, has something else in mind. I'm staying far away from it, man. I've a date with Suzie for the movies. She's more fun than getting drunk."

Now that conversation got my attention. Elfor and I were at least seventeen, but Rudy was barely fifteen. He didn't have any business going there if there was a lot of booze. I knew I had to find out, but who was going to tell me? Elfor? I doubted it. She hadn't been exactly honest anyway.

Maybe I should have paid more attention to what everyone was talking about. I went in search of Velma Hoyt. I'd neglected my other best friend while Darrell was in town, but she understood, about Darrell and me. She forgave the neglect.

I never stayed after school for what they called extracurricular activities. I had work to do at home in the fields. We, like all farm families, always went to town on Saturday. It was our time to buy groceries, maybe pick up a bottle at the state liquor store, attend the movie, or just plain stand around and talk with the other people you didn't see all week. I tracked Velma down in the dime store where she clerked on Saturday nights.

She practically hugged me, but couldn't because a customer walked up. When she finished she smiled at me.

"I get off at nine o'clock. Are you staying that late?"

"Yes, the folks went to the movies. Let's meet at Wilson's and get a cherry phosphate when you're off."

"Sure, when Darrell's gone, I'm the substitute date." She grinned wickedly before turning to another customer.

At ten minutes after nine, we placed our orders at the counter and grabbed the table in the back next to the jukebox before the people from the movies started drifting in.

"Why not sit at the counter?"

"Because, Velma, you're from town and I need to know what's going on. I don't want everybody to hear me." I stuck a nickel in the jukebox and selected a Glen Miller while the soda jerk brought our phosphates.

"What's going on at the junkyard at nights? Have you been there?"

Velma's built like me, on the stocky side, but well proportioned, sort of blondish, and when she answered, she blushed.

"Well, yes, I have, Elvie, but I quit going there. It just got too weird for me, besides I could be in real trouble if Sheriff Eikenberg or his deputy came by. I'd lose my job."

I felt my eyebrows travel upward. "Really, Velma?"

"Really, Elvie. They drink too much, but that's not the only reason I left. They're talking about celebrating Halloween in the old way."

She saw the puzzled look on my face and continued. "That's when everybody dances around the bonfire. The boys were asking about whether they had to wear costumes and Tom told them not to bother. Clothes weren't necessary. I think that was just booze talking. Don't you?"

"You may be right, but what else does he mean by the "old ways?"

"I'm not sure. Like I said, it just got too weird. That was two weeks ago and I haven't been back."

By this time the music was dying down and teenagers in bobby sox and farmers in their Saturday clothes, some dressed in overalls, and their families started coming in. I patted Velma's hand.

"I think you made the right decision."

I did not confront Tanya on Sunday. I waited until Monday and took the car into school so I could visit the library and do some research. What I found in that book about witchcraft turned my stomach. They not only danced around the fire, but they chanted all sorts of things. The one encyclopedia said that it was all imagination, and they just thought they were summoning the devil. The other encyclopedia said they were actually honoring the pagan gods and not summoning up demons. Either way, it didn't strike me as anything normal. I didn't know whether to ask Tanya or talk it over with Pastor. And Halloween was this weekend. Since I was young and didn't want to hurt Tanya's feelings, I stewed about it all week. Now I know better, but as I say, I was young.

Before I knew it, Friday, the last day of October, and I still hadn't talked with Tanya. I kept telling myself it was because we were harvesting and there wasn't time, but Friday after we were off the bus, I made time. Tanya wouldn't talk about Halloween on the bus, and I felt I knew why. We got off at the Swenson lane. It meant I had a mile-and-a-half to hike on home, but this was important.

"Well, Elvie, are you going with me tonight?" Her blue eyes were dancing with lights. "We would make such a team."

"That's what's worrying me. According to what I read, in the 'old religion,' you're dancing around without clothes on and you're honoring the pagan gods."

Well, what of it? People were doing that thousands of years before the Catholics showed up. You know as well as I do the Lutherans didn't show up until the sixteenth century."

I know my mouth dropped on that one. Pastor had been very explicit during catechism. Luther wanted to return to the worship practices and rituals of early Christians. Luther was questioning what he felt was man's doctrine overriding the words of the Bible. He hadn't meant to start a religion based on his name.

"You're distorting everything we learned, and you know it! You can't possibly intend to dance without clothes on. Your whole family will be hurt if the word ever gets out."

"You are such a prude, Elvie! You are afraid to learn what people have practiced through the ages no matter what the persecution. At least Rudy's not like the rest of my family or you. Most of my family, as you call them, are as big as a stick-the-mud as you are. If you change your mind, you know where we are. It's a chance to experience new things."

Tanya marched off without a smile or a backward glance. Did she think I'd follow her and apologize? As it was, I had three choices. I could go home and forget about her, I could go to the junkyard tonight, or I could enlist someone to help me.

My mind and stomach churned. Little Elfor, how could you change like that? This was going to break Anna's heart. How could I explain things to Darrel? Now that brought me up short. Darrel wasn't the oldest, but he was definitely the responsible one and always protected the younger ones. He wouldn't want either Tanya or Rudy there and would have done something to stop them. But I wasn't Darrel. Rudy wasn't going to listen to me anymore than Tanya. My parents wouldn't understand this any better than the Swenson family. The sheriff wasn't going to pay any attention unless I could convince him kids were drinking booze and I couldn't even tell him what kind. It looked like there was only one person to turn to, but first I had to do the chores.

I flew through the milking and separating. Then it was putting away the milk and cream, washing the disks and the body of the separator, and hurriedly cleaning myself up by supper time. That's what we called dinner then: supper.

I barely slid into my chair before grace was said. Once everyone had a helping of food, I asked my father, "Would it be all right if I took the car into town tonight?"

"Isn't the football game at Kimbleton this week?"

"Yes, but I want to see Velma." That wasn't exactly a lie. I would like to see her.

"I'm sorry, Elvie, but your mother and I are going over to Peterson's tonight. Didn't your mother tell you?" Well, maybe she did, but I'd forgotten.

Needless to say I took a flashlight and gave thanks that it was an Indian summer night and not frosty, chilly cold like in could be in Iowa this time of year as this was a three mile walk.

Pastor Hagendorf was a short, powerfully-built man with blue eyes that would glow with love when preaching a sermon or they would turn ice blue when someone (usually teenage boys) got out of line in church. He loved to ring the church bells and on Sunday morning he would emerge from the tower red-faced and huffing from the exertion of pulling the rope for over fifteen minutes.

Mrs. Hagendorf showed me into Pastor's study after I insisted it really was important enough to interrupt Pastor while he was laboring over the sermon for Sunday.

"Hello, Elvie, this is a surprise. Have a chair. What's troubling you?"

I could feel my cheeks burning and my stomach was in knots. I slowly sat in the chair and admitted, "Pastor, I need help." I took a deep breath and plunged into the recital.

I know it sounded strange, but suddenly it was all out. How Tanya believed that Tom Pyke was her real father. How Pyke was luring the young people in with booze and strange tales. Tonight they intended to dance around a bonfire without benefit of clothing.

"How do you know all of this?"

"I was invited by Tanya. She said I was a prude. She left out the part that I am a Christian."

Pastor smiled at me. "I'm glad you trusted me, Elvie, but you must admit this is difficult to accept. You may be wrong."

I must have got what Mamma calls my stubborn look as Pastor stood up. "However, on the possibility you are right, I think I'll check it out. If you are wrong, will you apologize to Tanya?"

"Of course."

"I didn't hear a car. How did you get here?"

"I walked."

"Then you'd best come with me. We'll check the junkyard and then I'll take you home."

Silence reined in the car as we headed for the south side of Austin where the junkyard was located. By 1952 most of our roads had changed from dirt with deep ruts to smooth, packed gravel and speeds of forty-five to fifty miles an hour could be done without bones jarring or teeth rattling. Of course, boys would take the roads even faster and there had been some horrendous wrecks.

It must have been close to nine thirty when we pulled up at the front part of the junkyard. We could see the bonfire in the back part of the yard. Pastor looked at it for a while and then carefully removed his suit jacket, folded it, and put it on the backseat. Fires weren't unusual in the fall, but they were mostly during the day when people burned the extra leaves. We walked into the yard between the piles of scrap, tires, bottles, and what-have-you, but as we drew nearer we could hear chanting.

As we rounded a circle of piled up tires, I saw one of the strangest sights I've ever witnessed. What Tanya had told me was true. There were about thirteen mostly young people, all devoid of clothing, chanting some sort of nonsense about a harvest moon. They were dancing and jumping around the fire. I couldn't tell if their faces were flushed from the fire or from drinking. Tom Pyke was sitting on a pile of tires wearing some kind of patched together cape beating on an upturned bucket with an empty beer bottle and swigging out of a wine bottle. Well, I just stopped dead in my tracks. I wanted to look away, but I couldn't take my eyes off of all those nude bodies. I'd never seen anything like that.

"What do you think you are doing?"

Pastor's voice rang out in full form as he strode towards the circle. "You are breaking man's and God's law here. Rudy, Tanya, Bill, your parents will be your earthly judges. Repent now!"

Tom Pyke rose and swaggered toward him as the line came to a stop and several of the young people bolted; Rudy among them.

"Well, lookee, here. I don't remember inviting you. This is a private party." Tom waved the bottle in Pastor's direction. "As for breaking man's law, I don't see no police." He laughed, gurgling in his throat. "And as for God's law, I thought we were doing a damn good job of honoring it. You are the interlopers."

Tom dropped the bottle and made his hands into fists. "You're an old man, right? Let's say about fifty or fifty-six. I'll let you take the easy way out." The man was laughing, a wide smile across his face.

"That pretty young lady can stay though. She'll make a nice addition to my coven."

Well that woke me up. One thing I wasn't and that was pretty. Not ugly mind you, but no one would ever find me attractive but Darrel.

Pastor was walking forward to meet Tom, his right index finger pointing at the man. "Thus sayeth the Lord: Get thee behind me Satan." And then Pastor's hands were into fists and he slammed his right fist into Tom's laughing face.

For a minute Tom stood there swaying and then dropped to the ground like a stone; a skinny pile of bones and meat covered with that patched up cape of all different colors.

Pastor turned toward the gapping crowd. "Put your clothes on."

Silently the group obeyed him and slunk away. Somehow in the confusion Tanya had left. Was it when Rudy ran? I don't know. I just know she wasn't there.

Pastor had drug a hose up from somewhere and was putting out the fire. When it died down he used a piece of metal and scraped dirt up around it. By this time Tom was sitting up cross legged, looking bewildered at the turn of events. Pastor threw the metal plate on the fire. The moon and stars were bright enough to light everything around us, but it was growing colder. Pastor looked at the man on the ground.

"I suggest you leave here tonight. The parents and brothers of those young people are going to be really angry and they'll take it out on you. Elvie, it's time I took you home."

We were driving up the lane to my farm when I dared ask the question that was plaguing me

"Why did you have to hit him after using God's word?"

Pastor grinned at me as he pulled to a stop. "Elvie, God's word disposed of the spiritual evil, but it still left the man as a contender. God takes care of the spiritual; man must deal with his physical realities. Any more questions before I have explained everything to your parents and why I needed you as a witness at the Police Station.?"

I had no more questions that evening and I have none now. Tanya and I had gone our separate ways. Her parents sent her to Ames for college and I waited for Darrel. We visited whenever she returned to the farm, but our closeness was gone. Today proved that again. She had her beliefs and I had mine. Anna's death was the last time anyone in Austin ever heard from her.

To Seek Man

Deeton adjusted the scanning probe. Once the male came into focus, she locked in and headed down. The male grew larger on screen. His arm was upraised, his hand clenching the spear, his muscles rigid while the desert wind whipped his blue cloak against his full athletic body.

His sturdy legs were bare and this allowed Deeton the opportunity to appraise every aspect of the well balanced creature. He was a glorious example. How had OraCom known to predict this land and that male so exactly?

The Sisters had not consulted the OraCom for centuries. They had no need of its predictions. They had the sperm banks. Who needed to seek a man?

If only Acta hadn't indulged so liberally while consuming that Krenlian buzz liquid. She had remained under its influence while hallucinating for days. No one minded. Acta had muttered such fantastic rhymes, spouted the most hilarious tidbits of gossip, and had offered all manner of ribald observations on the ways of the ancients.

They thought the effects had ended after two weeks, but Acta had become obsessed with finding a male and imitating the ancients. She had searched for a man, ransacking each and every chamber in her section. She pulled out costly equipment in a mad frenzy. She was put into restraints and sustenance withheld. Medical ran a feeding tube down her throat.

One month later, she begged to be released. She assured everyone that she was sane again and did not want a live, physical man. Sperm was good enough for her.

For two days she had tended to her duties perfectly. Then while everyone slept, she crept into the Biosphere and wrecked four centuries of waiting, frozen sperm. It was a disaster for our people. Only one male child had been allotted to breeders this century and there were but two Sisters carrying. Both of their embryos were female. Our race would end with the death of the youngest.

All formed a solemn line behind the Great Mother as they approached the unused OraCom chamber to present their petition. The Great Mother unlocked the door and everyone followed her into the room. There was silence while she presented the petition.

"Where in this vast universe is there a compatible species of similar genetic composition and coloring?"

The wait began. Two days, then three days passed. Everyone had abstained from food and drink except for water. Most chose to speak in whispers. On the third day, the Great Mother emerged and called us all together.

"OraCom has given the coordinates. She has blessed us with selecting one Warrior to accomplish this task. Deeton, you are the one!"

Deeton had squared her shoulders and bowed low. Before leaving she had bid family and friends goodbye. Then she sped across the lonely places.

The male standing below was suitable indeed to fill the depleted sperm banks, and maybe, just maybe she would be granted the privilege of procreating in the olden manner.

There were wild tales of barbaric rites that once had been practiced. Hadn't Acta expounded on them? There were also reports of other star systems where beings still practiced going to a secluded space together and the man and woman doing things to each other. Deeton wondered why this thought always raised her curiosity and a desire to experience this sensation just once.

Deeton checked the scan for any intruder. There were just the two below her; the male and the smaller creature he had been pursuing. Was the second a child? Both were staring upward at her ship.

She noted the man's wide lips, crisp, curled hair, wide shoulders, and muscled torso. She hoped everything else was in proportion. The other appeared female, but was (amazingly) lighter, more of a bronze color. The hair was dark and straight, and although the mammary glands were large, the creature was grotesquely short.

The sand swirled around the ship as Deeton landed. She lowered the lift and then adjusted her working tunic. The male and female spread themselves at her feet as she stepped out. The female was making strange noises. Deeton dissolved her to end her misery. It was obvious the female was going to be forcibly taken as a mate. She had saved her from a great deal of distress. She prodded the male body with her boot.

He quivered, the muscles contacting in the most fascinating way. She used his spear to lift his head. His eyes opened and he must have realized that what had appeared from the heavens was a woman taller than he was. His eyes were liquid black, the iris was almost as dark as the pupil, but his facial skin had turned an alarming shade of gray underneath that healthy black skin. His eyes rolled, and he shook his head.

"Allah, have mercy," wailed from his throat.

It would be easier to stun and levitate him into the craft. The technological gap was too much for this primitive. He would have to be restrained during the journey. Perhaps suspended animation was the best option to avoid any injury to his necessary body parts and internal functions. A pity, as there would be no chance to become acquainted, and he would have been the first of his kind to see his world from above.

* * *

The welcome was all that Deeton had anticipated. The Great Mother was there to greet her. The Great Mother's massive body was gloriously clothed in shimmering red. Her many daughters stood behind her and were carrying all her emblems of power.

"You, my dear space traveler, may watch the awakening by my side. Your name will be with those chosen to mate with him."

Deeton's long journey had given her an opportunity to reflect on how childbearing would interfere with her space travel.

"Great Mother, I have been honored sufficiently by your attendance here and welcoming words. All those that mate with him should be from the proven breeders."

The Great Mother frowned. "It must be someone stalwart like you. Our Medics have determined that his primitive ways might induce him to be violent with a weaker mate. We do not wish to frighten him by obtaining healthy sperm by other methods. We want him alive and healthy for several years."

The Great Mother turned. "Follow me."

Her command included Deeton and the crowd left the pavilion and surged down the wide halls into his sleeping chamber. Everything was hued a soothing pink, and it was lit by pink crystals.

"All this is to relax him," someone muttered.

A younger sister could be heard giggling.

Medic Abbe waved her hands for attention. "Quiet everyone! He's coming out of the cryonic induced sleep. We've inserted a transchip for his lingual patterns to match ours."

She bent her cropped, dark head over the male while intoning, "Wake now. There is no danger here. You will find companionship and peace."

The powerful figure stretched and sat up slowly before looking around the room. His jaw sagged at the sight of so many females.

"Can you stand?" Abbe asked.

He nodded and swung his bare legs over the edge of the bed. He extended one foot, and then another before standing.

To the assembled crowd he was a delightful example of maleness. He was at least six foot tall and there was no apparent atrophy from his imposed sleep. His breath, however, was coming in short jerks.

"Good, good," muttered Abbe, and looked at him with a smile before continuing.

"We are your new companions. You have been given the privilege of selecting one of the younger Sisters for a guide while you accustomed yourself to our ways."

The male searched each face. "Where is she? That miserable woman I was chasing? My master will be angry if I don't bring her back."

"Master? You have no master here. We wish to be your friends."

"I must return her." His tenor voice was firm, filled with determination.

Abbe looked at Deeton for an explanation.

"I left her there on that miserable planet. She was not suitable and there was no room."

"Of course, a good decision, thank you, Deeton." Abbe turned back to the male.

"You see, nothing can be done about it now. She isn't here. Do you see anyone that you appreciate?" She waited, anxious to be back to her studies.

The male continued to look at them, his eyes finally focused on an opening in the milling crowd. They could see his muscles bunching as if to run.

"Perhaps it would help if we introduced ourselves. Then you could choose."

He shook his head while snarling, "No, no."

Abbe continued as though there had been no interruption, the force of her words commanding attention.

"I am Medic Abbe. This is our Great Mother. You will respect her and give her homage. Tell us what your calling is."

He bowed and raised his head. "I am Chutta, third high eunuch for Ibn Sina's harem."

Amelia

It was Duke's fault. Why else would he, Will Perkins, be driving over this Godforsaken back road just to reach Perkinsville on Halloween with the rain and fog creating havoc with his vision? He cursed the rain and Duke's invitation that re-ran in his mind like a bad dream.

"Hey, ole buddy, you've got to make it back for the big shindig. It's a family re-u-ion we've all been planning. I've got two pigs for the pit, and a joke that you won't believe!

"Aren't we just a tad old for Halloween pranks?"

"Naw," Duke's voice cut him short. "What's the difference between seventeen and thirty-seven? Shit, man, remember the time we put the outhouse in the hotel lobby?"

He had tried to break in, "I don't think the law would be so lenient with grown men."

Duke's voice buried his objections. "And the time I spent all summer making friends with Old Duggan's vicious hound, just so we could put the manure spreader on his garage overnight?"

Will was laughing. Damn, it was good to hear his cousin's voice again. The last time had been an argument over Duke setting up a gravel extraction business on the old Todd property. He could see the lanky frame, blue eyes filled with vitality and wickedness, surrounded by a pair of jug ears. "I've outgrown crapper humor, Duke."

So have I, so have I. This is far more elaborate."

"Well, what is it?"

"Uh-uh. It's enough to know it's someone who deserves it. To appreciate it, you have to participate in everything: Hug Aunt Tillie, shake hands, bless the young'uns, and drink some shine."

"No hints?"

"Nope, just do your best to arrive shortly before midnight.

"See you, ole buddy," Duke continued, "and hey, don't forget, that last stretch, five miles out of Perkinsville, is still haunted."

"Not that old, drunken tinsmith still wandering around?"

"Naw, we're more romantic now." Duke drawled the words, using two syllables where one would do. "This is a female type with a long, black cape, party dress, and laced up shoes."

"Hoo," Will snorted, using a comeback he thought buried with his lost drawl.

"Will, I really need you here before midnight."

"Well, it has been awhile."

"Right, you ain't been back since your maw passed on. Do you good."

So here he was, thirty-seven, brown hair thinning, body still lean from jogging, hunched over a steering wheel, trying to peer through the dark gloom and pelting rain while listening to some clown on an all-night country-western station singing about being his own grandpa. The windshield wipers kept up a steady swoosh while the headlights probed over a blackened road awash with water. He could almost feel the ancient trees hanging over the road and hoped the wind that was swirling the fog away hadn't blown down any limbs.

At least the road was paved. It was a definite improvement over twenty years ago. The Arkansas ground was still warm and the cold rain brought huge, billowing masses of fog that created its own surrealistic world. He kept the BMW at a steady pace, but did not speed. He still had three hours before midnight. The big shebang of the Perkins family should not be without its last namesake.

The rain slackened to a mist and the wind blew the rest of the fog away. Will began to relax as the bare roadway became more familiar. Just before he trounced the gas pedal, the headlights outlined a figure ahead.

Will slowed the auto to take a better look. Whoever it was would be drenched and cold. He wondered briefly why the person had chosen the wrong side of the road and brought the BMW to a stop.

He rolled down the passenger window and called, "Need a lift?"

The first glance came as a shock, but he quickly regained his senses as he realized this must be part of the joke. The woman was dressed in a long, black cape, the hood covering her hair. She leaned forward to look at him and then sighed, "Yes, it's no use. I cannot find my way."

She straightened and reached for the door handle while the wind whipped the cape against her. The dome light cast its glow over a hauntingly lovely, oval face. As she swept back her hood, she revealed an enormous amount of chestnut hair elaborately coiled around her head and large, brown eyes surrounded by thick lashes. She closed the door and turned to him, favoring him with a slight smile. "This is most kind of you."

She is, thought William, one foxy lady. Strange, she wore no makeup that he could discern and her clothes were designed for an 1890's party. She sat quietly, gloved hands in her lap.

"I'm going to Perkinsville. That's only about five more miles. Do you live there?"

She seemed to start. "I walked too far. Perhaps, if you drive slowly, just before town, about a mile I believe, you could let me out, and I can try again."

"You mean the old Todd Road?"

"Yes." She stared straight ahead, her hands relaxed in her lap, yet her body was upright and stiff, her face expressionless.

He eased the car forward and asked, "Do you mean that someone actually lives down there again?"

"In a manner of speaking." She stared out the window trying to see where they were. She offered no other explanation.

Will was puzzled. The old homestead belonged to him, but he wasn't sure what lease arrangements his lawyer might have made. From nowhere, the fog swirled up around them again. As he slowed the car to adjust for visibility, the answer hit him.

Duke's admonition to arrive just before midnight was part of the hoax. This was Duke's joke and he, William, was the patsy. Okay, Duke, he thought, let's just see how far you're going to carry this one. Instead of an old man that vanishes, Duke had provided a lovely female. A much nicer arrangement, and with luck, he, William, could turn the tables.

"Is there anyone expecting you?" he asked.

She twisted her hands in her lap. "My parents have been expecting me since I left." Her low, husky voice could only be described as anguished.

"Have you been gone long?"

She nodded and sighed.

"Will the welcome mat be out?"

"How I pray that they welcome me, but who could blame them if they did not. Ah, sir, if you but knew the grief that I must have caused them." She sighed again and continued to stare at the road.

Suddenly the wind whipped fog across the highway obscuring the glowing lights from the town ahead. "Look, there it is!" She pointed to the almost hidden road. "Please stop."

He pulled the auto over and turned on the dome light. She turned and extended one hand in a graceful, old fashioned motion. The dark eyes brimmed slightly and her cheeks were brushed with the redness of natural modesty.

"I can never repay this debt." She smiled and opened the door. Suddenly the skies unleashed a deluge of pelting rain. It washed against the car and the landscape, its roar almost drowning out the low sounds of the radio.

"Wait," he commanded. "This weather is too foul. I'll drive you there." The BMW nosed its way on to the graveled, unmarked road. They jolted along in companionable silence for about ten minutes as the radio grew fainter and fainter.

Will slowed the auto to better search for the old bridge that he knew would not bear the weight of this automobile. Fog seeped up from the damp ground and made a ghostly outline of Todd's Creek. From overhead came the click of branches arching over his car. Damn, he thought, I'll throttle Duke when I see him.

Suddenly, the headlights illuminated the rocks piled before the bridge and the weathered sign. Without reading it, Will knew it warned all that the bridge was unsafe to cross.

"I'll check it out for you. That bridge might not be passable." He reached across her and rummaged in the glove compartment for a flashlight. "Excuse me," he said as he turned the auto off, took the keys, and opened the door.

A quick scan of the bridge told him the old bridge was beginning to rot. The sides hung askew, partially gone. Most of the planking seemed secure enough to support human weight if one watched their footing. He walked back to the car.

"Is your house far from here?"

"No, not far at all. Is it safe to drive over?"

"Certainly not. Look, I can't believe anyone lives out here."

"I know," she agreed. "I expected everything to be changed by now. Perhaps, if the fog were heavier," her voice trailed away. She closed her eyes, shuddered, and then lifted her head. "Yes, I must go on."

She turned to Will. "Thank you again, kind sir." She adjusted the hood and stepped lightly out of the car. "You have my gratitude for your kindness."

Will was perplexed. What now? Was the party at the old mansion? Surely it was too decrepit for anyone to use. He placed a restraining hand on her arm. "That bridge is unsafe and you'll ruin your dress and shoes."

She laughed softly. "Where I am going there are far more clothes than I shall ever need and soon this will be an excellent road. Papa put it in when he built Todd Manor. He did not wish to bear the brutality of the so called 'civilized' world any longer, but dreaded going without its luxuries. At times, it has been lonely, so very lonely for Mother and me." She lowered her eyes and then looked directly at him. "Goodbye, I must hurry."

Will watched her for a minute and shook his head. Built Todd Manor? Either Duke had paid one hell of a price for an actress or the woman was mad. He punched the smart key to lock the automobile, and ran after her, the boards creaking under his steps.

The fog was still swirling as he caught up with her near the end of the bridge. He tucked her right arm under his left and said, "If you will allow a stranger to make sure that you come to no harm, I'll accompany you the rest of the way."

"How can I refuse so gallant an offer? I am Amelia Kaye Todd."

"Will Perkins, great-grandson of the founder of yon metropolis." He waved his arm in the general direction of Perkinsville. "Population per the 2010 census is now 1,500. William Todd Perkins the IV is the full title," he finished lamely.

He heard the sharp intake of her breath and laughed. "Did you, like I, flee the dullness of such a bucolic setting? And like many, now find the big city not quite to your liking?"

She sighed, but did not answer. They continued to wade through puddles and wet grass as there was no gravel. The fog billowed from the ground to meet the cold mist. My God, thought Will, we'll get lost for sure. I haven't been this way for over fifteen years. Todd Manor hasn't been lived in for thirty: too Victorian, too antiquated, too lacking in modern conveniences. His lawyer had sent an offer to purchase from a couple wanting to restore it; one more reason for accepting Duke's invitation.

"Let's stop for a minute to get our bearings," he suggested.

They stood silently, the fog swirling in ever thickening circles until it was impossible to see. He could feel her trembling against him, leaning on him, drawing strength from him. It gave him a sensation of sensual delight. The women he knew in California scorned leaning on a man. He took her in his arms to comfort her.

Suddenly, the fog released them and the moon slid overhead. The wind sharpened and knifed into his bones. He could feel Amelia shivering. "We should go back to the car and warm you. Our clothes are soaked and you are cold."

She pushed away, shaking her head. "No, no. It must be here, tonight!"

Amelia ran forward and pointed. "Look, look, there are the lights!"

From out of the darkness Todd Manor suddenly appeared, windows lighted with muted yellow. "And there, just to our right, see? It's the road and now it is newly graveled."

Will blinked. Who could possibly be in Todd Manor? Why would the road be graveled when the bridge was impassable? Unless Duke's trucking business was so profitable he could afford to put in a road from Graham's Cliff.

"See, there must be guests." The desperation in her voice emphasized every word.

"Why?"

"There's always a party during Halloween; a costume ball usually. People come from miles away and stay for days."

"That custom must have started after I left."

"How long have you been gone?"

"For years and more years. I went to Stanford and after graduation I bummed up and down the Pacific Coast on different jobs."

"Your parents were not distressed?"

"They couldn't figure me out." He admitted. "They died thinking their only son was a failure."

They began walking on the graveled road. "How long have you been away," he asked.

"I'm not sure. If everything is the same, it will be three years. Everything has been so strange. You might not be so kind if you knew my history."

"I can't imagine anyone being anything but kind to you."

She squeezed his arm, ever so faintly. "Thank you, but I must tell you the truth."

She hesitated and then began a halting, painful recital. "You see, I was lonely and willful. Once or twice I happened to glimpse a young man across the bridge when it was foggy. We began to meet on the bridge and he would tell the most outlandish tales of another world, inflaming my passion to see new things. "I should have realized that he was far too bold."

"That October was warm, misty, and foggy and the guests for the masquerade were few. There was not one person my age. In my disappointment, I had a terrible quarrel with Father."

She sighed. "After the quarrel, I ran out into the rain. I ran and ran until I crossed the bridge. The fog was so dense I could not truly see the changing landscape. When I came to what should have been the main road, I did not recognize anything and realized that I was terribly lost."

"I did find the young man in the town, but by then I was totally frightened. Everything was so different: The architect, the clothes, the modes of transportation. I was terrified!"

Amelia sighed again. "The young man let me live with him, but contrary to his promises, he would not marry me."

She bowed her head and wept. Then she looked up at William to search his face. It was as though she expected disgust or revulsion to be there.

"What else was I to do? That world was so alien. Every Halloween, I've tried to return, dressed the same as when I left, but until now the fog was missing. This is the third time, but how long that has been for my parents, I do not know."

Her monologue ended and Will was puzzled. He found it hard to believe that Duke would go to such lengths for a joke. Where was the slapstick humor? How had he developed lines for an actress with the speech of a bygone era?

"Was your friend a tall, lanky man with jug ears?" Will asked.

"Oh no, he is of medium height and very muscular."

Will could not believe her explanation, but decided to continue the charade. "If your leaving was so abrupt, are you certain your parents will welcome you back? Older people have been known to be a-ah-stuffy about such things." He hesitated to use more descriptive words as this young lady had not.

"They truly love me. Even if their hearts are hardened, I must let them know that I am alive and well."

Will studied the three-story home with a wide, front veranda. It was lined with pillars that supported a smaller, upper porch. All the windows were glistening with a mellow, yellowish light. They left the road that curved to the barn and outbuildings and took the path running between the box hedges towards the house. Shadows and scents from the rose gardens and flower beds greeted them. Smoke curled from the many chimneys.

Amelia's body became stiff and she walked with odd, jerky steps. Not once did she slow their pace until they moved between the decorative lanterns lighting the way up wide, sweeping steps between two huge stone urns.

Will sniffed. My God, kerosene! Didn't these people realize the danger of fire? He raised the knocker and banged it against the door.

"I wonder if they'll be able to hear us over the music." The waltz melody drifting out to their ears was like Amelia: old-fashioned. Twice more he banged on the door.

Suddenly, the huge panel swung back to reveal an old man dressed in an outdated butler's uniform. His broad, dark face expressed disapproval from the quivering chin to the wrinkled, hairless brow. Still, he strove to be polite to a stranger knocking at the door. "Can I help you? Do you-all have business here this evening?" Like the people Will remembered, the voice was husky while it drawled every word.

The butler peered at them and Amelia stepped forward. "Wilson, would you be so kind as to inform my parents that I have… "

She was interrupted as the old man threw his arms around her. "Miz Amelia! Praise the Lord!" He stepped back, embarrassed by his outburst, but he continued to hold her hands as though afraid she might disappear again.

His shouts had brought others running and the first to appear was a tall man dressed as George Washington. "Dear one," he cried as he swept Amelia into his arms. George Washington was followed by a plump woman dressed in a satin gown and powdered wig. Tears began to stream down her pink cheeks and her fake, white curls slid askew as she too held and hugged Amelia.

"Dear friends, you must excuse us. Our daughter, Amelia has returned." He choked, gulping on his words. Both parents kept their arms around her waist.

"Papa, Mamma, this is Mr. Perkins; Mr. Perkins, my parents, Mr. and Mrs. Todd. Mr. Perkins was kind enough to help me return. I'm not sure that I could have found the way alone."

"Of course," said Mr. Todd. He turned questioning eyes on Will, not sure that Will was "proper." Amelia's explanation overrode his reluctance and politeness and form won out. "Wilson, serve him something."

To Will he said, "If you will wait, we'll talk later. You will be handsomely rewarded."

Wilson led him to a small, waiting chamber and brought a hot toddy. Will sipped the drink and wondered why all the old style furnishings looked so new. They had to be reproductions he decided. The logs crackling in the grate drove the chill and wetness from him and he puzzled at the strange turn the affair had taken. What was the point of this joke? Why hadn't Amelia disappeared like a proper ghost? Why hadn't she laughed at him for his cupidity and where in the hell was Duke?

The band continued playing waltzes and songs that he had heard his grandmother play and he became bored. He picked up a periodical from the Victorian spool table.

He glanced at it idly. *Harper's Magazine*, November 1894, slammed into his eyeballs. With growing unbelief he flipped the pages. Henry Mills, Editor, proudly presents the new serialized installments of du Maurier's *Trilby*. The pages were crisp and new. Will dropped the magazine on the floor and sprinted towards the front, practically upending Wilson who was balancing a tray of drinks.

"I've got to get back!" he yelled at the astounded, old man. He ran out the front door and raced down the path under a now clear sky hung with a golden, harvest moon. A few leftover clouds were rapidly spinning into webs of nothingness.

His feet crunched down the newly graveled road and flew over the new planking on the bridge. He leaned against the upright railing, staring into the empty moonlit roadway for his BMW. He gasped air into his lungs, waiting for his heartbeat to subside. Again and again, his eye swept over the empty road. The wind touched the trees and flitted through the bushes, creating soft night rustles. Somewhere an owl hooted. The sky was a brilliant pattern of countless stars that should have been haze-covered. Everything was wrong; terribly wrong.

Why were the trees so immature? From their height, they could be no more than ten-years-old. Someone had recently planted them to mark the way to an important house.

Will walked forward, jingling the keys in his pocket for reassurance. Was this Duke's joke? Steal the car? How? Use a tow truck? Surely, there would be some sign of heavy equipment in the wet gravel. He had walked about a city block when he realized the gravel had thinned, and his tennis shoes began to sink in the soft muck.

"Damn," he gritted out between clenched teeth. He turned and looked for the bridge. At least it was there. It was evident that someone had graveled lightly up to the bridge and heavier once over it. Why?

He stood and listened to the night as he had done as a child. Nothing. The sounds of music from the house could not travel this far. He could hear the singing of the creek rushing over rocks and the mocking chatter of a squirrel. Somewhere a cow lowed, but there was nothing, nothing mechanical. He was undecided. Should he go back to the house and wait for Duke's explanation in the morning? Would the people there explain Duke's perversity? The sound of a train wailing in the darkness broke through his questions. Mournful it was: a mournful, crying wail from his youth.

"My God! They tore out the tracks when I was ten!" he shouted into the empty night.

Once again he was gasping for breath. He and Duke had bothered the work crew for spikes, for ties, for rails, and for attention. They had listened to the male joking despite the dire threats from their parents. Once they hauled one of the wooden ties home and hid it in his uncle's barn to use in a joke later. Suddenly, he realized he was freezing as an icy wind whipped through any open space of his light jacket. The temperature must have dropped ten degrees since he first stepped out of the car. Behind the hills a dog bayed, adding to the lonesome tugging at his core.

He trudged back to the house, his world spinning and shifting away from him. What, he wondered, would be his welcome this time? Duke's joke, whatever it was, couldn't match an ending like this.

Wilson put him in the attic with an eiderdown feather tick and lent him an old dressing gown with a promise to find more suitable attire in the morning. "Mr. Todd requests the pleasure of yore attendance at breakfast, suh," said Wilson as he closed the door.

Will sank back into the soft feathers as the twenty hours of driving nonstop forced sleep on him. His dreams were of unending grey cement roads and a lovely, brown-eyed Amelia smiling at him until awakened by Wilson in the morning.

"We are most grateful for your kindness to our daughter." Mr. Todd was dressed in a conventional 1890's morning suit and on his feet wore congressional boots. A spare pair had been found for Will. Mr. Todd laid his knife and fork beside the plate and poured another cup of coffee.

Will extended his cup for a refill. Breakfast had been ham, eggs, biscuits, gravy, fruit, and freshly made breads, jams, and jellies. He had done justice to them all.

"At least you are not the low, base cur who lured our daughter away," Mr. Todd continued. He upped his eyebrows as if to ascertain Will's character by looking.

"Sir, I can assure you that I never set eyes upon her until last night." He almost said 'until I picked her up' but wisely refrained. They had breakfasted alone in a small alcove. A buffet was laid out for the rest of the guests, who wandered down in twos and threes. Amelia he had not seen.

Mr. Todd set his cup in the saucer. "There is evil in this world, sir. That is why I withdrew my family to this remote area. Still the devil's work spread its darkness over us for a while. No matter as she is safely home. Since you were instrumental in returning our dear daughter, there is your payment to consider.

"Mr. Todd, I want no payment. I simply want to find my car and go home."

"Ah, yes, but for you, Mr. Perkins, where is home? And what is a car?"

"I believe you would call it a horseless carriage." Will wondered how much Amelia had told the old gentleman. Mentally, Will shook his mind. Why was he talking and thinking in their confounded way?

"From what Amelia has told us, your car is quite unlike any vehicle we have seen in pictures, horseless or otherwise."

Will nodded. "That is true. What is also true, when I re-crossed that bridge last night, my car and belongings had vanished. Even the roadway and bridge were different from when we walked over it."

"Amelia tells a strange tale of a land more than one hundred years hence: A world rife with immorality and degeneracy, so godless that women and men desert their own children. Is this true?"

"Those things do happen, but we've done away with institutional orphanages." Will doubted his words would alter Mr. Todd's opinion of his world.

Mr. Todd shook his head. "And what happens to the children without parents?"

"Some are in foster homes or group homes that are paid for by the states, and, well, truthfully, a great many are on the streets and homeless."

"Are they fed properly? Do they learn a trade?"

Will considered. "I don't really know what happens to them." Truth required more. "A great many become prostitutes, male and female," he acknowledged.

Mr. Todd leaned back and folded his arms. "To me, your system is far more brutal."

"Perhaps it is, but this has nothing to do with getting me back to my own time."

"True." Mr. Todd actually sighed. "Do you know that Amelia was gone for three long years?"

Will choked on his coffee and quickly used his napkin. "She mentioned it had been three years."

"Of course, you could try again this morning. The whole episode is inexplicable." He held up his hand to stay Will's comment. "All I know is that she was gone and then returned. Somehow you, in place of that scurrilous dog, were able to bring her home. She assures me that you are a decent sort: courteous and hard-working."

Will coughed politely, "I, ahem, well, I try."

Mr. Todd leaned forward. "If you are unable to return 'home,' you are welcome to remain here and find or build a place at our little settlement. I need someone at the depot when the train arrives with our supplies. The last man departed some time ago. Wilson and his son have been doubling their work shifts for me. Unfortunately they and the few natives around here are unable to read or to write with any clarity; nor, can they cipher. You are literate, are you not?"

Will nodded, then stood and offered his hand. "Mr. Todd, that offer is more than kind. If I cannot find my vehicle this morning in broad daylight, I will return and take you up on the employment offer."

* * *

Bud knelt by the old, opened steamer trunk in their attic. It was metal with decorative applied metal flowers, fancy scalloped reinforcements along the edges, wood slats ran over the top and on the sides. The leather straps for carrying were hardened with age. The paint was still fairly decent and the inlaid wood inside was decorated with Victorian scenes and there was a special compartment for holding papers or jewels.

He replaced a pair of very expensive, worn running shoes from this century, some papers, a key ring holding a BMW smart key, and laid a fancy ball dress over the top of them. Then he picked up the last item: a 1910 photograph of a prosperous man and wife posing for a studio photograph. The old style clothing could not hide the identity of the man and a wicked grin slashed across his lean face.

A yell from below brought him out of his reverie. It was his wife Shirley and her voice was becoming louder and closer.

"Bud, yoo-hoo, Bud! The sheriff is here. He wants to talk with y'all. He claims he found Cousin Will's car down by the old bridge. He says it could be foul play. Bud, do y'all hear me?"

Bud tossed the picture in and closed the lid, snapping the buckles upward. Then he stood and gave a thumbs up sign.

"Thanks, Cuz, you just helped me pull off the joke of the century. I'm just sorry I couldn't tell you all the details, but you left me no alternative. As the nearest next-of-kin that gravel pit is mine."

Still smiling, he turned and walked toward the narrow stairs.

"Be right there Shirl. Tell Dean not to get his self in a tizzy."

The Jewel In The Kitchen

Flame Mouth realized he needed a new home when he returned from hunting and discovered three man creatures in his cave boldly putting his Treasures in their leather bags. Flame spumed from his mouth and engulfed the interlopers.

While he chewed their charred bodies he realized if those creatures knew where he dwelt so did others. This area was becoming crowded with humans and their buildings. There was also the fact that four other full-grown dragons were living within 100 miles. It was getting harder and harder to find a decent meal.

If too many of these weak two-legs perished, armed hunters banded together to hunt down the dragon. They armed themselves with long bows and iron tipped arrows. They also used that instrument to fire the arrows rapidly. Craven died in such a hunt, his dragon skin unable to deflect the metal tipped arrows.

Flame Mouth waddled over to the stone where he slept and surveyed his home of five hundred years. It was filled with his precious treasures. He could not carry them all while hunting for a new domain. He would need to place as many as possible in the huge golden (really brass) pot and carry them with him. If he chanced upon another dragon looking for a fight he would lose all his precious jewels. The thought was horrifying; almost as horrifying as losing it bit by bit to the man creatures who would surely return.

His pale green eyes grew wider. How many had he already lost?

Flame Mouth spent the night counting his trove. He was red-eyed and bleary by morning's light. Those unspeakable, detestable, weaklings had carted off at least five hundred of his treasures and the amount of golden lumps from flaming the golden coins were fewer in number. Only the largest lumps remained.

Quickly he used his front clawed feet to scoop up as many jewels as possible and dump them into his pot. He used his mouth to grasp the handle and drag it to the cavern's opening. He balanced on the edge, turned and flamed everything left in the cave. Unfortunately, yesterday's meal consisted of those three scrawny creatures and his flame was not successful in melting the jewels or remaining coins.

He stretched his wings, grasped the handle again, and flew into the morning sky. He would need to find a place to hunt, but before that he must hide his jewels.

During his journey, Flame Mouth flew west by southwest leaving the bleaker peaks of his mountainous home. He had stayed close to where jewels were easy to find; whether on travelers or those massive stone buildings that housed the man creatures. Hovels he had ignored. Their inhabitants possessed no jewels.

The lands he crossed were mostly lush with greenery and large land beasts. Food was ample and so were the dragons. He needed a nice warm cave close to people who treasured jewels and gold, and dragons were few. He had flown for weeks when he faced his biggest challenge: A huge expanse of water.

There were a few islands and then water and more water. He flew for forty-eight hours before he found a resting place on an island. Exhausted he collapsed in a too small cave and curled around his pot.

In the morning, he found unknown fish in the shallows and scooped them up. He flew inward to find fresh water and other game. The water he found, but many of the fish were larger than the animals. This was a horrible place for a dragon as there was little game and few people. Worse, the inhabitants wore brilliant flowers or craved bone instead of jewels. Rested and fed, he resumed his westward flight, now heading slightly north.

As he approached the coast of a large land mass, a massive serpent of the sea rose to meet a huge, brilliant blue, flying dragon. Flame Mouth did not stop to watch, but headed north as rapidly as he could. He did not wish to risk losing his jewels.

He chose a high peak and landed before looking back to see if one of those large rivals had followed him. What the two-legged ones called an archipelago had appeared where the combatants had fought. Both were resting, glaring at each other. Flame Mouth assumed they were glaring. Both had wounds that were bleeding. The water serpent rose to strike again, but the dragon flew off to the south.

I will go north and then west, Flame Mouth decided. These dragons are too close and too foul tempered to permit another rival. Besides the buildings were small and made of mud bricks.

The other side of the mountain range proved delightful. The greenery was lush, the buildings higher, and large deer, felines, and bears were part of the edibles available. He made for a smoking mountain and searched the area around it until he found a comfortable cavern. He sank down on the stone floor with a huge sigh. Tomorrow he would hunt. Then he would investigate the places he saw. They looked small compared to the palaces of where he had lived, and yet, some of the buildings to the south were huge. One stone complex around a clear lake looked promising. He would scout it out by night.

Great stars filled the sky when he awoke. He snorted, stretched, and tried to blow flame. Only smoke emerged from his mouth. Not good. It had been a long, wearisome journey with too little food. Tonight he needed to hunt, but first he took time to fly over the stone city. A procession was winding around the main plaza and heading for the temple. He presumed the highest, most impressive building with a steep stairway leading to the top would be the temple.

Flame Mouth felt the saliva flowing and his heart pounding. The men in the procession wore helmets of gold and all seemed to be wearing huge golden earrings set with some sort of blue-green stone. He would return once his strength was back.

It took three weeks to regain his full flame and strength. Fortunately, this land was filled with large and small game. The inhabitants here grew gardens; not as large as where he once dwelled, but large enough to supplement his diet. He kept a close watch on "his" city. His scouting and hunting did not turn up any other dragons. This was a new land (dragon wise) and it was his. He sent a huge flame outward to burn any vegetation around his cave. He wanted a clear view if two-legged ones tried to invade his home again.

One evening while carrying a bear back to his cave, he saw an encampment of men. They were armed with spears and stone weapons. How delightful. This place did not have the weapons of his homeland. Since they were eating without a fire, Flame Mouth assumed they were going to attack his city. Let them. It would weaken everyone concerned and he could swoop in and take what he wanted.

The next day, Flame Mouth hovered high above the city while watching two groups of fighting men. They were too busy trying to destroy each other with their stone axes and spears to look upward. It was pathetic compared to the men in his original homeland. They threw flames, or huge stones from machines. They also aimed arrows at each other. These men, however, didn't let stone weapons stop them from killing and maiming. He noted that many of the prisoners had their hands cut off. Finally, he grew bored with watching and spreading his wings went into a downward trajectory while blowing his flame. The red flame reached out and felled the men milling in front of the walls and outer buildings. Flame Mouth flew into the city where these creatures lived and blew flames at anything that moved. Women and children ran from the buildings screaming, the weaker hovels collapsed, and Flame Mouth was left with a problem. Which of these buildings would house the treasures? Taking golden helmets or rings from a few individuals would not restore his lost treasures. In frustration he let forth another blast.

The blast knocked down another wall, There sat a huge clay pot large enough to throw in the golden helmets and the scepter he had seen in the dirt. He solved the problem of slowness by biting off the heads and spitting the helmeted heads into the pot. He would empty it when he returned home and use his teeth to extract the heads before using flame on the gold. Perhaps the heads of these people would be a delicacy like those of his homeland. When the pot was filled, Flame Mouth gripped the pot with his front feet, flapped his wings and rose into the sky.

Once he was home, he turned the pot over and out fell heads, scepter, a cascade of white bulbs on twine, other bulbs of unknown jewels or plant matter, and a man creature clutching a string of deep red jewels. Flame Mouth presumed they were jewels. Why else would the man guard them with his life? This presented a problem. If he directed his flame at the man the jewels would crack and be useless.

The man dropped to his knees.

“Oh, Exalted Master of the Skies, spare this poor, humble cook and I will prepare your meals for the rest of my miserable life.”

“Why would I need anyone to prepare my food? That is a man thing.”

“Brilliant Green Scaled Master of the Air, you have missed something man values above jewels: a properly prepared feast.”

Flame Mouth studied the creature. His black, coarse hair was cut short in front and clubbed back into a long tail. The brown body was clad in a white loin cloth with a coarse, bloody tunic over the upper body.

The man took advantage of the silence to continue. “It is fortunate that I was carrying the bowl filled with the necessary ingredients for a huge feast. All I need is the meat and the wood to cook it. You will be able to experience why men fight over the ground that will provide them with the delicacies for their provisions. Exalted Monster from the Skies, think of what you have been missing.”

Flame Mouth’s eyebrows had elevated. He had seen men and their female companions gathered at long tables being served on golden plates. Was it possible the gold was worth less than what they consumed?

"Why would they value it so highly? Do they expend gold to create food?" His voice rumbled out of his huge chest, wisps of smoke accompanying the escaped air.

"It is said that they pay gold and turquoise for the finest of flour to serve with it, and gold to buy the chocolate beans to make their ceremonial drink, Oh Master of Flaming Death. I do not have the ingredients for the drink, but I promise you a meal worth your glorious existence. All I lack is the meat.

"If you will permit me, your humble servant, to hunt for a deer or another large animal, a dish worthy of your Magnificence will be served to you tomorrow."

"You will not leave this cave. You are to remove all the jewels and gold from those heads. It will be less trouble for me to eat them. In the meantime, I'll dwell on what you say. Now get busy or you will be my first mouthful."

Quanto, the chef, began to shake and fell to his knees. One look at Flame Mouth's baleful eyes impelled him to begin the bloody task.

Flame Mouth ate each head as they were tossed aside. Finally he went to the opening and flapped his wings before lying down.

"Any attempt to leave and it will be your last. I'll hunt in the morning. If your food is not all that you claim, you will be my dinner tomorrow."

Quanto spent the night alternately shaking from cold and hunger. Towards dawn he fell into an exhausted sleep until a blow from Flame Mouth's snout woke him.

"Wake up you miserable creature. Here is the deer you wanted. Why I've listened to you I do not know, but I will permit you to prepare my food."

Quanto bowed. "Thank you, Exalted Beast from the Skies, but before I start there are certain functions nature demands of me. If I could but step outside…"

Flame Mouth's roar negated any necessity to go outside. Quanto bowed again.

"It would be better if the hoofs, horn, hide, and entrails were removed. Perhaps there is a knife in your other caldron."

"Another ploy to protect yourself, but it won't work. Frankly, I don't mind a few entrails, but this should eliminate the hoofs and horn. Rather indigestible, you know."

Flame Mouth bit off the legs and horns before spitting the offending items out of the cave. "Now get to work."

"But Glorious Slayer of Men, I will need wood for the fire. If you would permit…"

The roar shortened his words again.

"I shall provide the fire. One more delaying tactic and you are my snack."

Quanto bowed and struggled to heave the white tail deer into the pot.

Flame Mouth reached over and picked it up between his teeth and dropped it in. The glare in his eyes proved there should be no more delays.

The chef hurriedly decided to throw in all onions. If this huge creature didn't care about entrails or fur, what were a few vegetable skins? He tried breaking the onions apart and began crying.

"This is called Dragon's Stew in your honor, Exalted One. It will taste better if I could but borrow a small piece from that cake of salt in the corner. It would add flavor."

Flame Mouth considered. "Very well."

"I shall also need water; almost a half of pot full." He looked at Flame Mouth's one eye closing and the baleful look in the other and hurriedly continued. "Once the meat is seared, the water will tenderize everything and blend the flavors. It is how I earned my keep at the palace of the," he hesitated, "the master of the outer region." He did not believe calling his now dead Master the Exalted One would be in his favor.

"And you will try to steal my jewels when I use the other pot to carry up water." Flame Mouth bared his teeth.

"No, Lordly Master of Carnage, never, but if you distrust me so, perhaps I could ride on your back. I am but a humble cook. Jewels are not for the likes of me."

"Let's see if you can hang on."

The cook ran up Flame Mouth's back and wrapped his arms around the scaly neck. The dragon grasped the handle of the emptied clay pot, flew down to the river dipped the pot into the water, and rose into the air to return to his cave. Quanto's face was as white as his loin cloth once was.

Quanto crawled down the dragon's back and gulped air into his lungs as he squatted on the floor unable to move. Finally his lips moved.

"Exalted Carrion, I must get some wood to create a flame to sear the meat in the pot. Once that is done, I'll empty the water into the pot and use less wood to keep a low fire. I'll also need stones to set around the fire pit. They are to hold the pot above the fire." He felt this should keep him alive for the next two days, if he didn't starve first.

"Silly creature! Do you think I'd fall for such blatant attempts to escape when I am Flame Mouth? How hot do you need the fire?"

"Quite high for a few minutes. If I could have a tree limb to stir with, I could stand on your back or the pot when it is emptied of water. There would be no need to leave if you could create a flame."

Flame Mouth gave one searing blast. For a moment Quanto feared the meat would be burned, but he stood on one of the rocks inside and looked.

"I need a limb to turn it over for the meat is still sizzling. The other side needs to be seared."

The dragon hovered above the pot and reached one clawed, front leg downward, flipped the deer, and gave another searing blast.

"Now the water," shouted Quanto. His fear that the meat would burn and become tasteless meant he would be devoured overrode his desire to speak only soothingly to the flying beast.

Flame Mouth poured the water in and it began to bubble from the heat the pot retained.

"This should give me time to procure wood for a low fire. It needs to boil, that is bubble for a few lapses of time, and then simmer for the time it takes for the sun to move towards the south before I attempt to shred the meat."

"Why would you do that? I gulp them whole."

"But Master of Flaming Death, the flavor will be more intense; plus, I really do need a limb to keep it from sticking to the bottom. As you rule the heavens, I should rule in the matters of preparing your food."

Flame Mouth flew towards the bottom of his mountain and plucked a fair size limb from one of the trees. When he returned, he tossed the limb to Quanto and quickly checked his jewels. They seemed to be intact; plus this creature had nowhere to hide jewels in a loin cloth.

"Please, Eminent One, it must bubble for a while.

Flame Mouth emitted a steady medium flame to bring pot back to a boil. At the cook's signal he lowered the flame. Flame Mouth's eyes became half closed and a low humming sound filled cavern. The cook took this time to make a paste out of the dried chilies and garlic. After two hours, the cook gave Flame Mouth a break as he pulled the meat, discarded the bones, and shredded the meat. The shredded meat, paste, and a small portion of the salt cake were put into the pot.

"Oh, Master of Death, if I could have but one-half a pot of water to keep it simmering."

Flame Mouth could smell the meat and onions, but now the other flavors added to the aroma. Perhaps this weakling knew what he was doing.

"Climb up on my back," he commanded gruffly.

Once again Quanto was sure he would die. He was surprised to realize he was back in the cavern and water was flowing into his culinary creation.

"Thank you, Great Slayer of Women and Children. Now if it could bubble for just awhile, then it only needs to simmer until the sun is directly overhead."

Flame Mouth blasted away to bring it to a boil before lowering the flame enough to keep it simmering for another two hours.

In the meantime, Quanto was set to work polishing the jewels. Occasionally, he would stir and taste the Dragon Stew. Towards the last he added more salt. Flame Mouth became more and more impatient, taping one of his talons on the stone floor and glaring at the cook.

Each time Quanto would give a sickly grin. As the sun glided directly overhead and the shadows shortened, he announced, "It is ready, oh Glorious Flame of Death."

"Harrumph! This better be as delicious as you described or you will be my next meal as inadequate as you are."

Flame Mouth picked up the hot pot and took a swallow. He set it down and let loose with a burp. Small tongues of flame erupted with the burp. His eyes lit up and he lifted the pot again. This time he took a larger swallow.

"Very good, whoever would have thought raw meat would improve with cooking?" He swallowed the rest of the stew and stepped to the front of his cave. There he let loose with a mighty flame. It flowed hotter, fuller, and farther than he had ever achieved.

"My dear, cook, you were the jewel in the pot. You are retained. When I die this will be yours, in the meantime you may sleep over there." He waved a claw at the stone floor.

Of course, Flame Mouth didn't mention that he would live for another millennium.

Auntie May

I am ready early. It's all I can do to keep from pacing until the helolimo arrives to whisk me over the land to the White House. They still call it that even though it's been gilded for years.

That nasty Perkins person practically snarled at me when she called to inform me of the arrival time. Then she softened and practically dripped honey. I knew then that he had walked in on her.

"The President said that you are to be given every curtsy, Auntie May." I knew she was clenching her teeth and really wanted to call me Nanny just the way "she" had done.

How could my precious Georgie ever hire someone like her? He should remember all the coldness and hardness embodied in a personality like that, but it doesn't matter now. In a few minutes, I'll actually be with him.

It will be for the last time for my age precludes any more adventures. Dr. Cromwell had administered a special medication to enable me to walk with some dignity. She'd also given me little pills to use for replicating the effects. There were more little pills if the medicine and excitement made my heart go too fast. It seems the pacemaker can be overridden by the dosage.

I had always realized that Georgie couldn't take time off from his professional life to call on me. Not that he ignored me. Oh, no, he always had time to call even if for just a few minutes. He is as thoughtful as he is handsome. You've all seen him. That leonine head of iron silver-white hair, almost like a halo around his face, his almost perfect features, his blue eyes brimming with intelligence and concern for all people, his broad shoulders and still athletic form, though I know he is nearing ninety-six.

Oh yes, he is a handsome man, but you should have seen him when they laid him in my arms for the very first time. He was so perfect, yet so comical. His large head was covered with soft, dark curls. His eyes were squeezed tight with three little lashes on each lid. Even then his shoulders were incredibly broad and his doubled fists twice the size of a regular baby. Only his legs looked scrawny, sticking out below his rotund abdomen.

I was in the room to take him home with his parents. They had hired me three months before and felt that the early bonding was important. I'm a certified Auntie May (now retired), registered with the Department of Health since 2080. Once I had held him close, the nurse put him in his mother's arms for the short ride through the halls and up to the parking level. When his parents entered the chauffeured helocar, she handed him to me. My precious little boy and I sat in the front with the driver. She didn't look at him for a week.

Both of his parents, in their own way, were proud of their handsome son, but they never really knew him. All they wanted to hear were his achievements. They were not concerned about his day to day existence; the dirty little chores, the sleepless nights. They could have afforded to purchase a Nanny from the assembly line, but they didn't want to hear the required robo account of daily activities. Plus, they wanted their son to be stimulated and to develop a caring capacity of relating to other human beings. For that they were willing to pay benefits and taxes on top of my wages. Both were aware their inability to connect with others. They were the product of such parenting. Their Nannies had been recycled from older siblings and allowed to continue functioning when their software programs were outdated. They realized my shortcomings in the language area as I am fluent only in English and Spanish, but they felt any child of theirs could overcome that during the years of schooling. How right they were.

It was her custom to call for him at six when they returned home from the city or emerged from their separate cubicles where they spent hours designing and implementing functional robots for industries. Then they would dismiss me.

Just what they did, I never knew until Georgie was old enough to tell me. Every week I submitted a record of his progress. When I informed them that he had rolled over at two months, they didn't believe me. When I reported he sat up at five months, they scolded me. When I told them of his walking at nine months, they threatened to replace me with a Nanny until he walked over and dumped his father's drink on the floor. They didn't call for him for two months. They wanted none of the experiences of growing children.

Little Georgie was always active. He was in and out of everything. It was as though he was possessed by a natural curiosity that made him need to discern what made things run or function. Then he would see if it would perform differently when altered.

There were times in those early days when I felt guilty about his clinging to me and would try to hand him to her when she called for him when there were guests. The older ones always cooed and ahhed over him. They recognized the combination of physical beauty and mental abilities. Once, when the guest was from a high ranking socio-political family, Georgie refused to be handed to her. Most embarrassing, but it angered her. I feared my job was in jeopardy.

The next evening when I took him to them in our little handover ritual, she said, "Thank you, Nanny."

"But I'm Auntie May." I was hurt, shocked, for we are an honorable profession and do not expect to be insulted by being called a hunk of plastic and gears.

Her lips and teeth smiled, but her eyes were hard and flat. "Oh, but how like the Nannies from the pre-robot days you are." Her voice was crisp and cool.

She was jealous, but not enough to hire a new Auntie May. That would have disrupted her time and might make Georgie cry and have all sorts of traumas. From then until he matured, she simply tolerated my existence.

The days of his exploring never really ended, nor his enthusiasm for climbing to the highest point. His blue eyes would take on a wicked gleam when a new obstacle needed surmounting; not truly evil, you understand, just wicked. He needed to see what would happen when he survived a challenge or knocked down an adversary. It's a quality he has never lost.

Yes, I protected him from himself in his boyish exuberance. She did not care. They just wanted the honor he would bring them as they aged. Such honor would enhance their standing in society.

My position ended when he was twelve and no longer called Georgie, but George. He was sent to a boarding school to prepare him for Harvard. There were times when we could visit, but they were rare. Former employers did not want the early childhood caregiver to maintain contact. They were frightened that the grown child would ignore them or the grown child loved Auntie May more than them. We corresponded regularly. How he found time I'll never know.

Once he made time for me to be on vacation with him. We spent a summer month walking in the cool, northwest forests, but that was many years ago.

I watched with pride as he went from lawyer to Representative, to Senator, to Vice President, and finally to President. Just think, my little Georgie, the President, has made a private appointment time for me. Everything is arranged. His favorite cookies are in my handbag, more are in a box. I know they'll take them away, but I don't think they'll take an old lady's purse with her medication. If they do, I've planned for that contingency.

It's strange, but as one grows older the built-in mechanisms of protection will work more efficiently. You realize how important it is to protect all those you loved and nurtured over the years; even when they don't realize you are doing this. It's the same thing as when you held their hands when they were little to keep them from darting in front of a landing helomover.

I check the time. Fifteen more minutes. I turn on the holovox for the news to see if I have been correct in my analysis. I dare not be wrong.

It is the same as yesterday. No one knows what will happen. Will President Raber use the new, untested weaponry against the Russians spreading over Eastern Europe, or against the Chinese spreading to the South and East, or the Sudanese overrunning all of Eastern Africa? Will the weapon spew radiation or just wipe out thousands and cause earthquakes and tidal waves across the Arctic Ocean area, Mediterranean area, and the Pacific Ocean?

Why are all these world powers pushing against each other? Why when the world has bumbled through this long without a major outbreak as predicted back in the 1950s? Why is the decision left to one man?

I dare not pace. That will expend what little energy I have left. I sigh with relief when I hear the buzzer.

"If you will come to the roof launching area, your helolimo is here." Dryer's awed, cracked voice lingers over the last syllables. Never in his years of servitude has a pensioner living in the high desert had a Presidential lift call for them. Wealthy citizens would treat an old Auntie, yes, but never anything so grand.

After I'm settled in, the helolimo takes off. It's difficult to see the world below. Heights always made me dizzy. The pilot is military and doesn't speak except to say, "This won't take long."

At the Presidential Pad, the attendant is waiting. She has been assigned to be with me all the way to the office. She is sleek and dressed in black from head-to-foot in the new style. The body is covered, but every crevice and crack is outlined. She raises her eyebrows at my dowdy shoes. Let her. I need to lean on her to save my strength.

Perkins looks the same in person as she did on the hologram screen. She's big with coiled blond hair and so much makeup one would think she's a hollow shell underneath. Her blue eyes appraise me and find me lacking.

"What is that?" Her voice is sharp and she points to my box done up silver wrapping.

"His favorite cookies. I made them myself."

She stares at me for a moment and laughs. "How quaint."

"Of course, you cannot take those in there. They must be analyzed. We'll let him know they will be given to the settlements." She must have saw the hurt in my eyes for she added, "He'll appreciate the gesture. Why on Earth did you bring a bag? I told you it would be confiscated."

"There are certain items I don't wish to leave in my apartment." My old lady's voice was quavering more than usual. "You never know who might break in, but mostly it is because of my medication. They still haven't replaced nitroglycerin."

"I thought you had a doctor's clearance."

"I do, but one never knows, the excitement I mean." I wait hoping that the plight of an old woman might sway her.

"The rules are that you leave the bag." Her voice was harsh. "Then I let you enter."

I entrust it to her keeping as she is no longer important for the escort is leading me to the door. She stops, taps at the door, and then she steps back, bows, and retreats.

The door opens and a man emerges and bows to me. He holds the door for me to enter. George is standing, waiting for me with his arms open and he moves toward me.

"My dear Auntie May! How good of you to come." He holds me close and I can smell his cologne and feel the still hard muscles in his arm through the black Commander In Chief uniform he is wearing.

He steps back, but keeps his hands on my shoulders and smiles at me. "It is so good to see you again."

I can see the shock come into his eyes at my aging, and I pat his arm.

"It's all right, Georgie, uh, Mr. President. I'm nearing 205 now. That is why I wanted to see you again"

He leads me to a chair. "Sit here, Auntie May. Was the trip too tiring?"

"Oh, no, it was exciting. Now I want to hear about your children."

"They are all grown and doing well in their fields. All that is except Aben, he's still in school, you know."

Of course, I knew. Everyone knew about his children, but chit-chat still exists.

"I brought you some cookies, but your guardian (I sniffed) insisted on analyzing them."

He laughed. He had drawn a chair close to mine and was sitting and holding my hand. "She's all rules and regs—that's Perkins. Now what about you? I've neglected you since my last marriage. Are you comfortable? Do you need larger quarters?"

"Oh, dear me, no, it's so confusing and exhausting to move, and really, I have more than ample space for my needs. I do thank you for asking." I gave his hand a squeeze, so warm, so comforting.

I looked up at him and swallowed. "It's all true, isn't it, Georgie? All those dreadful tales on the holovox. That's why you're wearing your uniform, isn't it. You're getting ready to give those orders. That's why you agreed to see me today, just in case, isn't it?"

He tried to laugh, but it was forced, and then that wicked look was there. His blue eyes were sparkling just like when he was little and there was another tower to destroy. I knew him, and now I know the truth.

"Dear, dear, Auntie May, you know better than to worry about such things. They'll back down this time just like they did before. Their claims of new weaponry are meant to frighten people like you.

"Do you hear from any of your other babies?"

It was his usual diversion tactic to take my mind away from what he was doing. I'm surprised he didn't ask for a drink of water.

I lower my eyelids for a while and then look at my darling, little boy grown so strong and so powerful. "You were always my favorite. All the rest were just employment."

Tears, unbidden this time, slide down my cheeks. "I only wish that I could have seen your children when they were little."

He withdrew his hand and shifted uncomfortably in his seat. "Now, Auntie May, you now my wives had their own preferences for their Aunties. It was their responsibility. I was always too busy to interfere."

I stretched my hand out to touch him one last time. "Oh, George, you can't possibly think that I'm rebuking you. You just don't know how lonely…" My breath comes in rapid little gasps.

"My pills—they're in my bag. Ms. Perkins has it—under her console I think."

My eyes are closed, but I hear him opening the door shouting orders. There is the sound of lots of scurrying feet on the marble and then silence as they must have crossed to the thick carpet.

"Where? Where?" He is shouting in my ear and he dumps the open bag and all its contents onto my lap.

I pointed to a little silver box and someone hands him a glass of water.

"No, no, it just goes under my tongue. Just a moment's rest, please, and I'll be fine."

"Of course, Auntie May." He is stroking my arm.

I hear Perkins snort before speaking. "Mandale is waiting, sir."

"Out, out all of you." Georgie is brusque and my heart is saddened. He is truly concerned about me.

He pulled his chair closer and sat holding my hand. I know he is watching me, and I slowly relax the muscles in my face.

"There, just a minute more and then I'll not take any more of your time. I know Mandale is your Cabinet Representative. I shouldn't have come." I smile at him.

My little Georgie smiled back. "Of course, you should have, Auntie May. When you return home, your apartment will be filled with roses." His smile grows wider. "You didn't think I would remember, did you?"

"You remembered just like I remembered you liked real chocolate." That was so touching, and I fumbled at the heap on my lap.

"Here, Georgie, these were for Dryer, my building's Secure Man. Ms. Perkins took yours and said they would go to the settlements." I smiled and winked at him just like when he was little and we would outwit "her."

"Real chocolate? Auntie May do you have enough credits for the rest of the month?"

"Oh, yes, Georgie, I do have enough. I've been planning this for some time."

In my mind, the resolve strengthened. I'd been planning ever since they said that neutrons could and would be activated by lasers if necessary. I know my Georgie.

He unwrapped one and bit into it. "Mmm, this is just like old times." His voice never betrayed how bitter it must be for I had laced them with all the extra pills the doctor had given me. My time is very short now. I will have no need for credits or the drugs.

He helped me to the door when he finished and I heard Perkins say, "They are all waiting for you now."

This time I had to lean on the Escort's arm. She had to support me all the way to the lift area, but I didn't care. The only danger of my plan failing would be if Georgie went to the doctor too soon. An analysis would show what was in his system, but I know my Georgie. He hates doctors. He will wait until he collapses and then it will be too late. Dr. Cromwell had been quite explicit about what would happen if someone with more muscular strength and lower blood pressure took the medication that made my old, decrepit body move normally. That person will die within the hour.

The Complex

Gavin watched the young couple eying the tower and the activity of the early buyers. Carpenters hired for the interior construction were hurrying in and out carrying tools and debris. Other buyers were still busy cutting or pecking out their quarters. The look of awe and wonder on the couple's face told him they were more than interested. It was obvious from the arrangement of her feathers that she would soon be nested.

Gavin sleeked back his stubby crest and checked his dark feathers. He was pure blue-black and a forward crest might frighten them. A toothy smile appeared under his hooked beak as he approached the two.

"Hello, my name is Gavin Darter. Welcome to the Complex. May I show you around? Then once we've toured everything, I'll be able to tell you about all of your options."

The man had red feathers, tipped with black. The woman had blue-green feathers that looked like jewels glistening in the sunlight. Too bad, thought, Gavin. Their young are all apt to be multi-colored. It would limit their earning abilities, but young people had no regard for color continuity.

"That's great. I'm Pilan Atter and this is my mate, Dilma Atter. We were wondering about the costs."

"You're jumping way ahead of what to consider as your costs when looking at a development of this scope. Notice that all of our towers were natural trees. Steel and cement are used to stabilize them. Our engineers have certified that the maximum growth is complete. The artistic bole like growths on the sides of many of them are natural. They add a certain architectural element to the entire project. At night the lights coming from the inside creates patterns at ground level. The entire area is an organic complex in keeping with the aims of our great leader. Our location means there are certain nutrients in the area that can be gathered at no cost. This eases any budgetary concerns when first starting out." His prompt didn't elicit any information regarding their finances and he continued. "The rocks in the background and in the foothills add landscaping and beauty." He waved his right wingarm at the towering landscape.

"Now you need to tour one of our furnished units to see what can be done with a little ingenuity and planning."

Gavin led the way up the tower to the fifth level. "I really don't recommend the lowest two levels." He lowered his voice just to the right pitch to convey concern. "The rain is carefully channeled, but there are no guarantees on the lowest two levels. Their initial cost is less, but your insurance would be extremely high." He did not mention that those were the units for affordable housing.

He opened one of the circles and stepped through and to the side. As he expected the young couple were awed. He knew the colors of blue and teal would be appealing to these two.

"This unit has the semi-circular sofa cut from the tree's wood. The same is true for the casual tables and two of the chairs. The table and sofa won't grow anymore as they have been disconnected from the bark.

"The recliner was purchased. Back here is the eating area and the hallway to the sleeping section." He hoped they noticed the finely woven drapes at the front window. He needed to mention it when they returned.

They followed him with an expectant look on their faces.

"How long does it take to create spaces in something this large?"

"It would depend on any tools or the number of laborers you can afford. I'll grant that you could do it yourself, but that would take at least two or four years. It wouldn't be in time, ahem, for any other addition to your family."

The eating area was smaller with a table and chairs for formal occasions and a counter for chopping. A deep blue, double sink was set below the upper cabinets and shone in the artificial light shining directly on it.

"I do recommend hiring an experienced cabinet crew to create your supply storage area. So many times the inexperienced have doors that won't open or close properly. At other times, the entire unit looks out of balance. The floors require the same expertise."

Gavin led the way to the bedrooms and nature chambers. "As you can see one chamber is here in the hallway for any guests or the second bedroom occupant. The built in hallway closet is for any extra supplies or materials you may wish to store." He opened the main bedroom door with a flourish.

"Look at that bed!" He let their eyes take in the twig bed fitted with a mattress made from the softest fluff of far-away cattail pods. "See how the vivid blue complements the curtains and the stained walls. The tables on either side are also made from real twigs. The enclosed wax holder is made from sheets of golden mica to enhance the color coming from your windows." He stole a glance at the couple to see their reaction.

The woman looked almost dreamy eyed, her lids halfway over her dark eyes. "Oh, Pilan, it's beautiful, but how could we afford anything like that? I mean we will soon be three and the other rooms will need to be furnished too."

Gavin refrained from looking at Pilan. He was sure the young man was embarrassed and he hurried to fill in any silence.

"These units are merely furnished to show what can be done. Very few of our buyers start off with such elaborate furnishings. Of course, we can always provide the names of our suppliers and crafts people.

"Why don't we look at the other room? It's furnished for just such an addition." He led them into the next room. It was better to keep them excited about the affordable necessities than the possibilities.

"Notice how the sun lights up this cheery room and the gorgeous beige and lavender lower wall runs up into the blue simulating the outside. It's a real child's room once the nesting is complete. This room only takes about two weeks to complete. It is something you would want to have ready." He cleared his throat and pointed to the smaller nest with fake twigs from the Riven factory.

"You'll notice the crib nest is manufactured by the Riven Company. It's sturdy for when they are small, but can easily be broken down and stored for the next one.

"Do you like the shutters that can transform this into a dark, safe place? Sometimes parents prefer that if the child has difficulty sleeping."

The couple looked at each other. "This is so much more than we anticipated. It would be the perfect home, but perhaps we should look at something smaller." Pilan had estimated figures in his mind.

Gavin looked at the young man. "Why don't we step over to the office? I can show you our plans, the cost, the amount you need to deposit, and compare that with what you have and what you plan to spend. You both look like the type of people we want to help get a firm start in life. I'm sure we can negotiate some points." He gave his positive assurance smile. "It doesn't hurt to see what your options are."

The couple looked at each other. "It really wouldn't hurt, Pilan. Then we would know what we are facing.

"Pilan's face darkened, but he nodded. "Yes, you're right. We don't really know what is required."

"Right this way." Gavin led them down the stairs into the fresh desert breeze. As they stepped outside, Gavin took a deep breath.

"Just smell the fresh desert air." Gavin didn't want to give them a chance to think. He continued to talk rapidly as they walked. "It's not like the city with its thousands and thousands of people. A complex like this will only have a few hundred; yet, you are within close proximity of decent jobs, entertainment, and there are places for children to play in safety here. At night you can look up at the stars." He motioned upward at the clear horizon and stopped in mid spiel.

"It's that damned dragon again!"

The dragon's red scales were sparkling like polished stone in the brilliant sunshine. It made a wide sweep over the area and then like a bullet swept downward. Horror was written on all three faces as they realized the dragon was headed straight for them.

"Follow me!" Gavin broke into a run for the office door. He turned in time to see the dragon rising with Dilma in his right claw and Pilan chasing after them.

Another dragon appeared on the eastern horizon and zoomed after the first, its huge wing span glistening pale green with smaller blue scales that gleamed like sapphires. His silver talons were fully extended.

Pilan and Gavin ran after the dragons with the workers following them. The dragons soared upward for the foothills of tumbled rock. The gap between the dragons had narrowed and the large green one flew over the other. The men tried to run faster, but the desert was draining them and they stopped when the red dragon dropped Dilma on a small patch of ground free of boulders and turned to face the newcomer. A roar came from two dragon throats as they met in the sky and tore at each other's wings.

Dilma was gasping and sobbing, holding her stomach area as she scrambled to hide behind the rocks rimming the area. She peeked over the top and watched the red dragon and green-blue dragon tear and claw at each other. The red dragon broke free and tried to flap away.

The green one closed in and grasped the red's extended wings forcing it downward. As they neared the ground the huge dragon veered upward, and then slammed the other like a bomb against the rose-beige rocks. The green and blue dragon flew to a rock near Dilma, flapped his wings, and trumpeted his triumph into the still desert air.

Dilma forced herself to stand and found she was not too badly hurt, bruised, achy, yes, but so far so good. How could she protect their unborn child against this monster?

The dragon was preening his scales and his sapphire eyes surveyed her.

"Well, why are you standing there? I'm not going to eat you. You're not big enough to be an appetizer."

"It's rather difficult to climb down in my condition. What if I fall?"

"You are of no consequence to me now that I realize it was your coloring that deceived me. You are not one of our young. I thought you had been captured, but you are a different species. Your wings are truly inadequate."

"There are more of you?" The thought of living in a dragon infested area was frightening.

"Of course, my dear, we need living space just as you creatures do. We migrated from a region covered mostly by water. Land resources were few. This area seems to have small game creatures. We are contemplating a move further north, but may remain here for a season while scouting other terrain. The other dragon was a surprise. Red dragons can be rather nasty and territorial just like you feathered humans, but we thought we had destroyed the red ones during the last war. Now I suppose the creatures chasing after us will have called out your militia or forces of some sort."

"I, I don't know. I didn't even know there were dragons around, but that salesman did."

"Does he know how many?"

"I wouldn't know, but you could ask him." Dilma pointed towards Gavin in the group of men approaching. Her heart seemed to rise into her throat when she realized Pilan was outpacing the rest.

"And who is that rash fool leading the pack?"

Dilma swallowed. It's my husband. He's worried about me."

"Hmm, husband? What does that mean?"

"It means we're married; mated. He's the father of my child."

"Aw, and he is proving how brave he is."

"No, he's proving how concerned he is about us."

"Spunky little thing, aren't you? Do you think you can convince that salesman to tell me about the other dragons?"

"Not from up here, plus, I think he is leaving." She pointed at Gavin's departing back.

"Do you mean the black creature scurrying back to that human complex?"

"Yes."

"If I lower myself, can you climb up between my wings and neck and hold tight? I believe it's possible to stop that cowardly cretin."

"I think so."

"Good, by the way, my name is Tao."

"I'm Dilma Atter."

The dragon knelt as Dilma pulled herself up onto his back. His skin was rough in this area, but there were no sharp scales. She bent low and grasped him around the neck.

"Not so tight. Tuck your feet under my wings. I won't be flying at top speed."

Tao rose and ran to the edge of the incline and launched into the air. He maintained a steady low beat of his wings until he was just a few wing spans past Gavin. A quick bank to the right allowed him to circle and land in front of the running Gavin.

Gavin fell to the ground and put his hands over his crest, certain this was to be his last day on earth.

Tao landed and knelt again. Dilma slid down and ran toward Pilan and was swept into his wingarms when they met.

"Shall we try to run for it?"

"No, Tao won't hurt us."

Pilan's beak dropped in wonderment, but then he heard Tao booming at Gavin.

"Arise you miserable creature. I need to know how many Red Dragons there are in this area and where they have nested."

Gavin pushed himself up to his knees. He didn't believe the danger was over, but if he could keep this dragon talking, he wouldn't be eaten.

"No one has located their nests. We aren't really sure, but we've only seen that large one lately. There was a smaller one, but it hasn't been spotted for a week. Perhaps it has moved on to new territory. At least that is what we had hoped."

"Enough. You are babbling. Which direction did they come from when attacking?"

"Ah, we were never completely certain. I mean we didn't have anyone one out on dragon watch. You are supposed to be on the other side of the waters. We thought it was a fluke."

"Did they attack anyone?"

"Uh, well, they did dive at one worker, but someone yelled and he jumped inside and everyone else managed to get into a building too. We thought they were just moving through."

"Bah! You are all idiots." Tao swung back to Pilan and Dilma.

"Did you two ever see them before?"

"Oh, no, this is our first time here," answered Dilma.

Pilan pointed at the mountains from where they had rescued Dilma. "I did see a flash of red come from that direction. I just didn't think of dragons. We had been assured that you were all across the ocean. Our kind do not venture near."

"Good. Your scraggly force of Eagles would be no match. We prefer the higher crags in real mountains. We ran those red interlopers away centuries ago. We thought them all destroyed when two Reds raided one of our lairs. I was assigned to destroy them. Once I've dispatched them, I shall return to my den. You creatures are simply too small for a sustainable menu."

Tao turned back towards the mountain and rose into the air. The flapping of his wings almost knocked Pilan and Dilma over. Awed, everyone watched as he disappeared.

Gavin rose and brushed the pebbles and dirt from his feathers. He assumed the chance of a sale to these two had evaporated and he still had a quota to meet. He had one more ploy.

"Perhaps you two would like a drink of water and a chance to rest after that harrowing experience?" His knees were still shaking.

"How many times have you seen dragons?" Pilan felt Gavin had lied about the sightings.

"Our leaders assure us that this area is perfectly safe. We cannot hide, and our Eagles aren't scraggly." Gavin felt they had to be reassured or they would raise an uproar when they returned to the city.

"They can't fly as high or as fast as dragons." Pilan was logical.

"True, but haven't you seen the latest technology? The dragons are a left over from the time of the devastation of humans without feathers. We will persevere." But his confidence waned as the couple walked away.

"Wait, we'll give you a tremendous discount!" It had occurred to Gavin that he could not let them take their tale of a dragon fight and the danger of becoming a dainty appetizer.

"Is that how you enticed the others to stay?" Pilan turned long enough to yell back.

Gavin ground his beak, but then he saw someone else pull into the lot. He hurried forward with a pull-the-beak-apart smile. He could still make his quota and the Complex would become a thing of wonder.

Depression Christmas

I was twenty-four when I learned that giving at Christmas time can be one of the loneliest acts that anyone can perform. Strangest of all, society would have called my teacher an ignorant, redneck drunk.

It was 1935 and Roosevelt was in office. Most Americans thought the worst of the depression was over. We were unaware of the total devastation the dustbowl was creating. My father had fared better than most. My sister and I were able to attend college where I met and married Tom Reynolds.

Tom was short, stocky, and confident of the future. His blue eyes gleamed when he told of new techniques to bolster farm production. The subject didn't enrapt urban me, but I loved him.

The day after graduation, a letter from the U. S. Department of Agriculture arrived appointing Tom the County Agent for Lawrence County, Ohio. Tom was like a madman. We poured over maps to locate our destination in Southeast Ohio.

"Come on," he urged me. "We have to shop and pack." We ignored the cold spring rain.

We stopped long enough to gurgle sodas before returning to my parents' house to finish packing.

My neighbor was horrified when she discovered where we were going. "That is hillbilly country. You will be absolutely buried away from society."

I had a cold, and protested through my sniffles and coughing. "It can't be that bad. I'm sure they have radio and a library."

My cold turned nasty and our plans for departure were delayed as pneumonia set in. Tom waited until after the crisis before leaving. Recuperation was a lengthy process. How I hated the mirror! I had lost twenty pounds, my dark eyes were dull smudges, and my face had sunken, white hollows were where cheeks should have been rosy. Doctor Jacoby finally gave his permission to join Tom. Christmas was but five days away. My bags had been packed for weeks and I left the next day.

The train ride from New York City to Columbus, Ohio was exhausting, but when I struggled off the train, there he was: My Tom! He was rumpled, unshaven, and smiling. We hugged and kissed the long months away oblivious to the scandal we created.

"You're so thin," Tom cried. "You could pass for the Ghost of Christmas."

"And you, why haven't you shaved?"

He laughed. "I was afraid I might miss you so I came yesterday afternoon. Then I overslept. Come on, I'll buy you a cup of coffee before we claim your luggage."

He kept up the barrage of words as he pulled me through the crowds. "Have you had lunch? I've missed that throaty voice of yours. Wait until you see where we live."

Within the hour we were ensconced in our Plymouth coupe and rolling over the smooth pavement leading southward. Gradually, the terrain changed from hilly farmland to woodlands of ancient age. There were still farms, but less prosperous. The pavement changed to gravel and by afternoon we were fighting deep, grooved ruts in impossible mountain dirt roads. Many of the trees had dark, leafless arms shrouded by the half-light filtering through the firs. Tom had his shoulders hunched. He used one hand to grip the steering wheel and the other to manipulate the gearshift. He was devoting his whole being to driving while we jolted from rut to rut.

"Don't worry. We'll be home before supper."

I shivered and pulled my fur collar tighter. Supper? Where had he picked up that word? For months I had planned our Christmas Eve dinner. Afterward we would be beside some cozy fireplace, laughing and exchanging gifts. Now that prospect looked as cold and bleak as the snow covered hillocks and trees. Tom's cheerfulness faded as I drew my coat around me and refused to talk as we pulled into town.

This town was better than some we had driven through, but it gave off an aura of dirt and hopelessness. There was an unpainted mill beside a railroad station, a grocery, three taverns, two gas stations, a garage combined with a blacksmith shop, a fire station that was once red, a county courthouse complete with jail, the proverbial small, white church with a steeple, a produce and feed store that was almost as dingy as the mill, a U. S. Post Office, People's Bank, a Woolworth's, two cafes, and a library. Except for the newly painted taverns, the bank, Woolworth's, and the courthouse built of brick, it was a dreadful, dreary place. Not Appalachia, but a close second. What few people I saw were gaunt and hollow of eye. Only one hand raised in greeting. The rest seemed hostile or simply preoccupied in staying warm in clothing ill-suited to keep out the winter air. I was bewildered and a bit frightened. How could Tom expect me to live in this half-civilized corner of the world?

Tom was unconcerned. "We're here," was his cheery announcement. "These people have lived here for generations. It'll be all right." His reassurance did little to quell my fears.

The residential sections fanned off into the hills. The houses ranged from two Victorian gingerbreads to shacks long washed of any paint that might have been applied.

Our home, considering the town, was adequate. It was a white-washed, two story house with a basement and a sagging front porch. The plumbing, I was to discover, was a holdover from the previous century. There was a chimney and I was certain there would be a fireplace, but, no, it was for the wood cook stove and red potbelly coal monstrosity set up in the living room.

We entered directly into the kitchen. A large, black hand grasped Tom's.

"Welcome home. You done brought yore purty Missus."

"Right, Molly.

"Honey, this is Mrs. Mills, only she insists that I call her Molly. This place wouldn't be decent today without her."

Bone tired, I murmured some type of greeting and collapsed onto a chair. Something was bubbling on the stove and a pan of cornbread was on the table.

Mrs. Mills pocketed her money and slipped on her coat. Tom was spooning something from the bubbling pot into another.

"Here, take this with you. What about some apples for your children?" He placed the apples in a small pail that was sitting beside the stove. "Merry Christmas, Molly."

"Thank you, Mr. Reynolds, and Merry Christmas." She seemed to be crying as she left.

I was appalled. "What is the matter with her?"

Tom stared at me for a moment before answering. "Without those beans, she and her six children might not have had supper tonight. She saved everything for the Christmas dinner tomorrow. I've had to take turns hiring someone otherwise it causes friction in town."

I straightened in the chair. I had not imagined living day to day with such poverty.

"You don't realize how bad it is here." His voice was bitter. "The Department wants me to tell the farmers how only one hundred and fifty dollars for an indoor toilet will help keep everybody healthy. Diana, these people don't even have two dollars, let alone... " He took a deep breath and turned.

"Hey, what am I doing? This is Christmas. Here, look what I have."

He rummaged in the pantry and held aloft a bottle of champagne.

"Tom! Where? How?"

"I badgered your father out of it before I left." He smiled. "Now set the table, woman whilst your man carries in the bags. We'll dine in splendor on cornbread and beans, ham, and champagne. Don't forget to throw more wood in the stove."

It wasn't what I had planned, but we were together. While we ate, we held hands across the oilcloth covering the table, and I told him about the plays, the latest films at the Paradise, and the newest books. Exhaustion and Tom's blue eyes kept me from running to the car and driving back to New York. There was time enough tomorrow to tell him what a coward I am, but I cannot live here.

After we cleared the table, Tom brought out our coats with a cheery, "Well it's time to go."

"Go? Go where? I'm exhausted and it's snowing." How could he be so oblivious to my feelings?

Laughter brushed my protests aside. "To church. Where else does one go on Christmas Eve? It's not far, but we'll take the car."

The snow drifted downward in huge, soft crystals that sweetened the air and gave an ethereal quality to the dark pines that filled the low mountains. Anyone else would have felt at peace. I, however, was desolate and my happiness during dinner dissipated.

The church was like none I had ever attended. It was white and had a steeple, but there any resemblance ended. A plain wooden cross was nailed to the front door. Tom opened the door to a room filled with hand-hewed maple pews. The windows were plain glass, frosted and decorated by winter snow. There was no altar area, but a Christmas tree was in one far corner and decorated with paper chains, stringed popcorn, and a few bulbs. There were even bird feathers on it. A lanky adolescent clad in a plaid shirt and jeans sat beside the tree on a wooden stool. He was strumming a hymn on a guitar. The other corner held a potbelly stove that glowed a dull red. A church member would try filling it quietly during the service.

As late comers, we slipped into the last bench near the door. A few people nodded. Others whispered, "Howdy," or "Glad she's here."

They were all poorly dressed by New York standards. From somewhere came the stench of bad whiskey. The air smelled of burning wood, wet clothes, mothballs, and people. The children were seated at the front and their giggles and shuffling feet could be heard. I was amazed at their number. How could such ill-fed people be so fecund? A hush fell over the crowd as the pastor strode out to the center.

"Brothers, sisters, and children," he paused to smile at them. "Welcome in the name of the Baby Jesus. That's why we're here tonight, to welcome Him. He came just for sinners, yes, for you and for me." Someone in the front row interjected an, "Amen."

The pastor's high voice, a bit nasal and almost singsong continued. "And tonight we're going to let our children tell us about that wondrous gift, 'cause that's the kind of faith we all need: Just like the little children. Let us pray."

As one the congregation bent their heads while the pastor's words exhorted them toward supreme faith and sacrifice. I noticed a drawling, slurring quality. Not really a Southern accent, but just enough to give it a lilt, and to my ears a quaint, picturesque sound.

After the prayer, the children trooped up to sing Joy To The World. Then the play started. It was intended to show how Jesus, the Babe of Bethlehem, was for the whole world past and present. They took turns being shepherds, crusaders, and early immigrants. Too many of the children had pinched faces and wore clothes that didn't fit. Their shoes flopped and showed holes. What I wondered, have they to be thankful for?

They, however, were like children everywhere. Some recited their lines perfectly while others hiccupped or waited for the prompter to fill in every other word. Periodically they burst into song. Things were progressing mercifully to a close when a girl of about ten walked up. Her plumpness and rosy cheeks marked her as different from the others. New oxfords gleamed under the costume of deliberate rags, and her tow hair glistened in a stylish bob.

"I'm a poor Little Match," she began.

The man in front of us lurched to his feet. "Thash my daughter! What's she doin' in thush rags?"

The source of the whiskey odor was obvious. His wife tugged at his coat sleeve with one bird-like hand while she balanced the baby with the other.

"Hush, Will, hush. Sit down."

"I'll not hush. She's got better clothes. Ain't no daughter of mine gonna stand up thar like that." He lunged down the aisle, reeling from side to side.

"Anna Belle, you come home with me. You too, Bill." He hung for a moment on a man's shoulder, straightened, and led the reluctant children from the church. He kept muttering about how his family didn't have to dress in rags. His wife carefully wrapped the baby and fled with them, tears streaming down her red cheeks.

The pastor tried vainly to regain momentum, but things limped to a close after that scene.

Just before the last song, the disrupter appeared in the doorway and handed a large box filled with brown sacks to the nearest man as he said, "Here, Jake. I made a mess of things. Pass these out to the kids."

His voice was still slurred and rough. I shivered with revulsion.

We did not linger long; just enough to say hello to a few people. The children were busy exclaiming over the candies, nuts, and real oranges found in each sack.

Tom wrapped a blanket around me before starting the car. As the car pulled away, I exploded. "Well, that man certainly ruined everything!"

"Who?"

"That drunk."

Tom started to laugh. "Diana, how many men do you know that can go home and in a few minutes make up just the right number of Christmas sacks while drunk? Plus, he would be contending with one very angry wife and two disappointed children."

I took some time to look at the snow's soft landscape before answering. "None," I admitted.

"Correct. He quit school to raise his brothers and sisters. Now he owns the general store. He's carried most of these people on his books for years. He has contracts to sell supplies to the CCC camps, and to the construction crew at the dam our Department is building. He wanted to give those sacks as his Christmas donation, but the Elders wouldn't let him. The people were too ashamed at not being able to pay for necessities. His shame had to equal theirs before they could accept."

Snow was falling faster, hissing steam as it hit the hood. Like the snow, my discontent melted away. I snuggled closer to Tom. That rough, acting like a drunk man had given me a gift too. I no longer looked at the people here with horror, or feared being here with Tom. Not when such adversity could produce a person capable of humbling himself for a gift of love to children.

Between

It started with the noise of a hard, cracking sound. Its power shook the house, rattled the dishes in the cabinet, and caused a power outage. It was eleven o'clock in the morning and most were at work. This is Southern California and tremors have to be severe before most notice. Those that heard it assumed it was an earthquake or a horrible accident. Some ran out of their houses, but could discover nothing amiss.

I tried calling my power company, but my line was dead. I knew other people were calling the power company to find out how long the outage would be. My cell phone was useless and I had no land line. I went to my auto and turned over the motor to hear the radio. There were no stations coming in whether it was AM or FM except one local AM station.

A man's voice sounded like this was an emergency. "Please follow these instructions. We'll bring you the latest updates as soon as we make contact with someone. Right now, no one is certain what has happened. We cannot reach the governor's office. There are no casualties reported other than heart attacks and a few scattered accidents when the traffic lights went out. The mayor is recommending you turn off all non-essential appliances being run by electricity. from generators as we do not know how long the fuel will last. All transmission lines are down. Repeat: Turn off all electrical appliances and lights. The hospitals will need fuel in this emergency. Keep checking back to this station with battery power if you have any batteries. Stay tuned for more developments." The station went dead.

How curious. I turned it off and stepped outside. Nothing seemed amiss. The street was still there; the lawns, the trees, and the skyline of downtown Palm Springs. One elderly man was out on the street. Now he was gesturing at the blue sky; his companion, a dog was switching its tail back and forth.

I walked over to the next block to see if Vance had any ideas. He works at web designing from his home. Before I was at the door he came outside with a perplexed frown.

"What's going on? Anybody have any ideas?"

"Not really, unless you think this is a reality show like that old Twilight Zone program when all the neighbors get edgy because only one can start their car." Vance paused and asked. "You want to chance it and start yours?"

"I already did that for the radio. Next time it will be when I head out for work."

"Mike, you'd better call first."

Vance always had to have the last word. I waved at him and returned home, shaved, and went to the garage. My car started, and I didn't hear any creepy music as I backed out, but the garage doors wouldn't close. Without electricity, the inside mechanism would not respond to the remote. I went back in and locked the kitchen door and reentered the auto.

The noon heat was verging on one hundred, but it was clear. Instead of the DVD I usually played, I flipped on the radio. It was strange. My satellite stations were gone.

"Now I'm ready for eerie music." I found myself speaking aloud and flipped the radio off. It was time to concentrate on driving the crowded arterial street. For some reason there were fewer people when I merged on to the I-10 heading west. I almost made it to Banning when the autos started piling up and a trooper was frantically trying to direct those that could to turn around and go back. I quickly pulled off onto the shoulder. What was going on?

The trooper walked up, disgust in his voice. "Mister, you can't park here. Go back while you can."

"What's the problem?"

"The road's gone. Now get out of here before I arrest you. You have my permission to drive across the meridian."

The number of cars was rapidly swelling, horns were honking, and people ahead of me were shouting. Since there were no cars coming from the west, I quickly drove across the meridian, and parked on that side. The trooper was busy directing everybody back. I got out of the car and ran forward. I looked to the south and the north and realized the landscape had changed. There were mountains in the distance, but these mountains had no vegetation and they were stark, bony-rock masses of black. I looked to the side and where there should have been vegetation and pavement there was desert: beige sand glinting in the midday sunlight. There was desert back behind me, but here? People had planted and cultivated crops; trees had been planted generations ago and they were gone. The skyline of Banning was gone.

I saw the trooper glaring at me and hurriedly returned to my car and drove back towards Palm Springs. I pulled out my cell phone and dialed work. Nothing, no sound, no robo voice telling me all circuits are busy, please try again later, just nothing. This was beyond bizarre. Where the hell was Banning?

Once I was back in Palm Springs, I pulled into a gas station. All of them had signs: Cash Only. Pay First.

I pulled up into the space in front of the mini-market and dashed inside.

"What's going on? How many people do you think carry cash?"

The dark haired, dark eyed cashier eyed me gloomily. "All the ATMs are down. So are our credit card systems. We're running on generators. No cash, no gas, or anything else."

I stared at her. "What does your home office say?"

"We can't connect with anyone. Look, mister, you want gas or not?"

I did a hasty calculation of the dollars in my wallet. There was barely enough to buy one meal out.

Another man walked in. "What the hell's going on around here? The phones aren't working, ATMs and credit purchases aren't working. How's a man supposed to get to work?"

The cashier plastered a tight smile on her face. "From what I heard, the job might not be there."

He stared at her and then glared at me. "Where's a bank around here?"

"About two miles straight down, but without electricity, it might have closed."

The man stomped out and another irate person took his place. They had helped me make a decision. I headed for my own bank. Surely, they had money for their depositors.

The bank, like many buildings in southern California, is a pink beige box with a column or two by the portal. The ATM had about a dozen disappointed people milling around, the drive-in lane was full and people were lined up by the door. I obediently took my place and prayed it wouldn't get violent. People were not in a good mood.

"Is there anybody in there?"

"I don't know. I can't see through the other door."

"Hey, don't shove."

"Watch it, dude."

A police car, sirens blaring pulled up to the back. Someone sent their kid to check on what was happening (probably under the delusion that an officer wouldn't shoot a child). The kid came running back.

"They said everybody has to leave."

The police marched up and one officer stepped forward.

"Folks we need this area cleared. We had an alarm from here. A dangerous person may be in there."

A woman behind the door used a large key. Her face was sickly looking underneath that professional hairdo and above the dark business suit.

"Thank you for coming, officer. My name is Karen Overton. There's no robbery, but the alarm was the only way we could call you. Someone is locked in the Safety Deposit room and we can't get it open without electricity. Our generator isn't starting. We can't be open without electronics and I'm afraid all these people will be as angry as the ones inside. I can't securely lock these doors without electronics either."

The officer's face had changed from annoyed to concern to stern to amazement with each of her sentences. "Okay, Ms. Overton. I'll send a man over to a locksmith's. Maybe he can think of a solution, and I can post two men until you get your generator up and running."

"But we need money. The damn ATMs aren't working," a man's voice yelled out.

The woman looked at him. "Sir, we've already dispersed the money we had available. We can't get to anymore."

The lights inside the bank blinked and turned on showing that the generator had started.

"Does the ATM work now?" Another voice yelled out.

"No, sir, just the inside.

"Officer, thank you for coming, but how do I get in touch with you when we run out of money again?"

He looked at her. "Lady, I don't know how you contact us. We don't know what's going on and we're spread thin with all the traffic accidents. You start to run low, just close it down. And don't let anyone else into that Safety Deposit Room until the regular lights are back. You're lucky I don't write you up for a false report." He motioned the rest and they returned to their cars and took off, sirens and lights blazing.

We were permitted to enter five at a time. An hour later, I walked out with $500.00. It was the maximum a person could withdraw and when their available funds were gone the doors would be locked. I wanted as far away from there as possible.

Buying gas for my car was the next thing to do and then groceries and maybe some water. Otherwise everything would be gone—if any of those stores were open.

I finally made it home by four p.m. The neighborhood seemed quiet and I rolled into the garage and carried my purchases inside.

I went back to the car and turned on the radio. The announcer was back on with these reassuring words uttered in a fast, clipped manner.

"Everybody remain calm. For some reason, the landscape out there has changed. There has been no communications with any of the rest of the United States or elsewhere. If there is an emergency, contact the local police or sheriff's office. 911 may not work. A command center is being set up at City Hall. Remember, another update thirty minutes from now. In the meantime, stay away from Palm Canyon Road. There have been three bad accidents."

Once again there was dead air and I flipped it off. To console myself, I grabbed some food out of the fridge and made a sandwich on the theory that I might as well eat it before it goes bad.

While I ate, I wondered what it looked like from up in the air. I pulled out my cell and used the speed dial to call a friend that had a small plane when I realized that was useless. I'd just have to drive to his place and see if he was there. I drove out to his home with a private air strip. This is Palms Spring, you know.

I could see Bret sitting in his office drinking from a can of pop. He had the door propped open for the breeze since the air conditioning was unavailable. The thought of a summer here without electricity is enough to panic grown men. I knocked at the jamb.

"Bret, it's Mike here."

"I can see that." He looked up and gave a half-hearted smile. "Out wasting gas?"

"Yeah, well, I tried driving to Banning. Everything's changed, dude. Have you been up in the air?"

"No, I'm thinking and conserving my fuel."

"Why? If you don't use it, the police are apt to confiscate it."

:"That's true, but so far, I'm not making any noise. If I go up, everyone will see me."

"Has anyone been up?"

"If the reporters or police have, they aren't saying much. Why did you come back?'

I recounted what I had seen while Mike listened intently. When I finished, he crushed the pop can and stood.

"Thanks, Mike. That confirms my thinking. It's what I was afraid someone would tell me, but I'm glad you're here. I can use your help."

"Sure, what can I do?"

"Help me by going up with me and turning on these two DVDs players. I was trying to figure out how I was going to do that by myself. The plane is rigged for plugging them in. I have it for when I take up paying customers and they need to plug in for whatever reason."

"No problem, but why are you taking them up in the plane now?"

"Harmonics, Mike, harmonics."

"Huh?"

"Harmonics have been around for a long time. Did you ever take advanced math or philosophy?"

"That would depend upon your definition of advanced."

Bret chuckled. "It started with the phrase 'music of the spheres.' That would be Pythagoras with his ratios based on music. Then during the renaissance, the theory really became the property of the greatest men in science when they searched for harmonies or harmony of the universe, if you will. It included people like Newton. The twenty-first century has brought us to the brink of cosmic harmonies. Mike, the harmony just got disrupted."

Bret hunched forward again to look down at his charts. "Something disrupted the tonal harmony. Somehow we need to be back in tune.

"I'm not a musician, although, I'm not sure this needs a musician. I think by duplicating their music, we'll be able to restore it. I've worked it out with certain formulas. I had started wondering about it last year."

"Bret, I don't know you were capable of that type math."

"I can to a certain extent, but do you know what you can do with computers now? I hooked two of mine together and let them work at night."

"Here's another question. Why didn't the entire world crack up?"

"Maybe it did, but I'm hoping it's just this section of it. From what you've told me and what the news has said, we are in a different time frame. We need to go back or forward in time. That's something else that needs to be resolved. It's as though time and space actually warped from the discord."

"So how do you know what tones caused it?" I tried to keep sarcasm out of my speech and hoped he'd take it as skepticism.

"I was listening to the same music as they were playing at the Coachella Music Festival. According to the announcer two bands were playing the same song at once on different stages. I've burned another copy of what I have. We're going up and play both at once. I'm hoping being up in the air, and having the sound turned way up will make up for the difference of not having amplifiers. If I'm right it should put everything back. It'll be a big help if you can push in both play buttons at once. I've already have the sound as high as it will go."

"So how does it get to the outside if we and the DVD players are inside?"

"Another detail I took care of earlier. I've attached speakers to the outside and run the audio cord back inside to connect to the players. I used layers of duct tape around the windows where the cord is threaded through.

"It should hold." He muttered after a pause. He probably saw disbelief on my face.

"It'll be all right, Mike." Brett grinned at me. "At least I think it will."

"What will be all right?"

He shrugged. "I'm hoping everything." He picked up the DVD players. "Shall we go?"

I'm not sure why I agreed to it, but what could be worse than the situation we were facing? There isn't enough land to support people with food. This is the desert and nobody but a few had gardens. People driving through on I-10 were trapped here. They'd be angry once the full perception of what happened hit them. Hell, they were probably angry already. I thought of that mob of visitors at the festival's center. That's thousands and thousands of people that don't live here.

Light planes aren't my favorite. The flooring between you and the outside world always feels insubstantial to me—like if I tromped hard on it the floor would break through and we'd be doomed. Following

Brett's instructions to use both the seat belt and the strap across the shoulder and chest didn't improve my worries. I pushed them out of my mind as Brett soared toward Indio. The airport in Palms Springs kept trying to contact him for a flight plan and to warn him. Brett ignored the radio.

As he neared the festival grounds he went higher into the thinning air.

"Get ready, Mike. Push them both when I say now."

We could barely see the edge of the RV Park and then we were over the staging area.

"NOW!"

I pushed both buttons. We both could hear that music; it was faint, but we could hear it. Brett kept circling the area until we could not hear any sound from outside. I looked down.

"They've played, Brett. Do you want an encore?"

"Sure, why not? Then I'll have to head for home."

The plane suddenly did a pitch and roll and then threw us side to side, rolled again while it seemed to vibrate. The vibrations were making my immobile body shake. Brett was hanging onto the wheel and trying to bring the plane back under control. Then it felt like something turned it upright and Brett managed to bring the plane around and head back towards Palms Springs. I wondered if my face was as white as his.

He flipped his radio back on as he headed went over his field and banked. The landing was fairly smooth considering the beating we had taken.

I didn't leap out of the seat once we were down. First I had to unbuckle everything. I wasn't even sure I could stand. My legs were shaky and I'm pretty sure I was gasping for breath. Brett opened his door and I opened mine before stumbling out. I was elated to be on desert sand again. It took several deep breaths for me to have sense enough to grab the DVD players and close the door.

"Let's head inside and see if things are back to normal."

As we approached the door, we could hear his telephone ringing. A wide grin hit Brett's face and he yelled up into the sky.

"We hit the right note!"

Morally Made

Michael looked in all directions. The New York City street was empty. There was no discernable movement around the small stores. The people in the automobiles were too intent on arriving at their destination to notice. He pulled out a square of white material, flapped it, and laid it over the stand that appeared and positioned itself directly under the material. The material expanded to cover the legs. He opened a chest, pulled out an array of fruit drink mixes, and laid them on the cloth. Next he pulled out a huge sign that read:

HURRY HURRY GET YOUR FAVORITE FLAVOR OF MORAL FRUIT MIX

This was New York City and his chances of finding a likely subject should be excellent. As day began to brighten, vehicular traffic increased and became a mass of crawling, dodging, beeping, jerking, stopping, and starting machines. People appeared on the street hurrying to their stores or small offices in the buildings. Some frowned at him; some mouthed "Good morning," but most ignored him.

Another vendor selling pencils and related items set up not far him. Michael decided to concentrate on the people approaching his area. He selected a well-built, dark-haired man wearing an expensive brown suit and carrying a leather brief case.

Brandon Dillard tried ignoring the stand, but a sudden overwhelming thirst tightened his throat. His lips were dry, and the urge to drink liquid made him stop.

"Pardon me, but do you have bottled water to go with those mixes?"

Michael made sure his brown eyes smiled as well as his lips. Earth humans responded well to such tactics.

"Why, yes, but it's only a couple of bottles for my own consumption during the day. One must stay hydrated, you know."

"Suppose you sell me one of those bottles, and then I'll buy three of your mixes."

Brandon really had no intention of using the mix, but felt the man would sell the water if he bought the mixes.

"Since it is the first sale of the day, I'll agree. That will be ten dollars, please." He continued smiling while Brandon pulled out his wallet and completed the transaction.

Michael pulled up a bottle and pointed at the layout. "Which flavor or flavors would you like, sir? I can assure you they are morally made."

"And what does that mean? A bunch of nuns made the mixes?"

Michael chuckled. "Quite funny, sir. No, I mean our methods are meticulous and no contaminants are in or on the fruits my company uses."

"Why not just say organic?"

"It seems there are many definitions of organic. Some of it is quite unsanitary." He shuddered and waited.

Brandon shrugged. "Just pick three."

Michael smiled and complied. He put the mixes and bottled water into a sack before handing it to Brandon. His work was done. It didn't matter if anyone else purchased a mix, but he would need to wait until nightfall to disappear.

Brandon opened the bottle of water and gulped it down. He stuck the mixes in his pocket before resuming his hurried pace. He needed to arrive at the conference room before nine a.m. Everything had to be perfect for his sales pitch. His usual take was several thousand dollars after paying expenses (if he paid them) before moving on to another city. Every night he drank a toast to the genius of Ponzi. He had updated the pitch, but Brandon liked to give credit where credit was due.

Night was falling when Brandon arrived at his hotel suite. He loosened his tie, slung his suit jacket over the sofa arm, and turned on the television. It had been an excellent day. He pulled out the makings for a strawberry daiquiri and found the mix almost empty. He frowned and remembered the mixes in his jacket. Could the man have thrown in a strawberry mix? There it was: Strawberry. He pulled out a pitcher that looked like a quart and threw in the mix and added water. The smell of warm, ripe strawberries hit his nostrils. Could it taste as good as the smell? He raised the pitcher to his lips and swallowed. The taste of fresh strawberries lolled over his tongue. Superb! He had figured the man as a lesser con man than himself. He poured a glassful of the mix and started to add up the checks and money.

Next morning, Brandon surveyed the new batch of "investors" seated in front of him. He went into his pitch as he tried to drive away the thought that he was robbing some poor grandmother of her nest egg. He needed their money to pay the caterer bringing box lunches. They should be grateful that he gave them dreams to dream.

"There's a matter of payment, Mr. Dillard."

It was the caterer, wanting his money before he distributed the boxes. Brandon put on his best smile, knowing inside he was morally wrong and about to lie.

"Normally, I pay everything at the end of the sessions. There's still one more day." He didn't bother to say, *I skip town before anyone receives money.*

Then Brandon noticed the man's frayed shirt and run down shoes. He remembered how hard his father had labored to keep them all fed.

"Of course, I'll pay you right now."

He opened his briefcase. "That is two thousand-five hundred dollars, right?"

"Yes, Mr. Dillard."

"There you are, and an extra hundred for good service."

"Thank you, sir, thank you." The man was practically bowing to him.

Sweat started to roll down Brandon's chest. *What have I done*? Still, it should keep the man from alerting the owner of this place that he, Brandon, might be a welsher.

By nightfall, his throat was dry from all the talking and he mixed the second packet of his purchases. How could a mix taste like fresh orange juice? He yawned. He needed to pack and get a good night's sleep as he meant to leave in a hurry tomorrow. He needed to stop thinking about all the people he was robbing. He hid his face in his hands.

"I need a vacation," he said to the wall. "I can't think about the people I've duped."

Friday's gathering was crowded. He smiled his most brilliant, dental-enhanced whitened smile and enchanted everyone. By the afternoon he was seated at the table, taking their money for investing.

"Mr. Dillard, thank you for this opportunity. My husband died suddenly and we never saved much. This gives me a chance to live a normal life." The woman was small and dainty, her face a cherub's face with lines framed by white hair, and his breath caught in his throat.

"Didn't Social Security increase your income?"

"No, it lessens it when one member dies. That is what happens to working people, Mr. Dillard." This speaker was a man, possibly in his forties, but his hands showed the brunt of hard labor. "There's never enough to retire."

"Excuse me." Brandon stood and ran from the place. What was he doing? He was stealing from everyone. How could he possibly repay anyone when he didn't know how many he'd bilked over the years? He couldn't remember their names. Could he find a decent paying job without stealing? In the morning, he would try.

Brandon did try, but he discovered there had been too many moves, too many fake companies, and no one to verify his previous employment; and still his conscience nagged him. Brandon found himself walking into a police station and pleading with them to take his confession. The police had no difficulty tracing his trail from city to city as people had filed reports of fraud. Crossing state lines meant the federal government filed charges. Brandon pleaded guilty. He was fifty-three when released from prison.

* * *

Michael was packing his mixes. No one noticed his chest and table disappearing as he picked up the white cloth. The passing traffic ignored him whether they were on foot or in vehicles. As he began folding the cover, a wrinkled, white-haired man in worn work clothes with determination written on his face stepped in front of him, his hollow eyes reproaching him.

"What was in those mixes you sold me years ago?"

"Morals, I told you."

"I'm ruined. I've been to prison. All I can find for employment is laboring in a warehouse."

"Congratulations, you have morals. The mixture was a success."

"But I'm broke and growing old!" Brandon was almost sobbing, and people began edging away.

"Remember, dear man, the meek shall inherit the Earth."

Michael finished folding his white cloth and disappeared.

About The Author

Mari Collier born on a farm in Iowa, and has lived in Arizona, Washington, and Southern California. She and her husband met in high school and were married for forty-five years. She is the Coordinator of the Desert Writers Guild of Twentynine Palms and serves on the Board of Directors for the Twentynine Palms Historical Society. She has worked as a collector, bookkeeper, receptionist, and Advanced Super Agent for Nintendo of America. Several of her short stories have appeared in print and electronically, plus two anthologies. *Twisted Tales From The Northwest* can be found online. *Earthbound, Gather the Children, and Man, True Man* are on Amazon.

Twisted Tales From The Universe
ISBN: 978-4-82414-172-9

Published by
Next Chapter
2-5-6 SANNO
SANNO BRIDGE
143-0023 Ota-Ku, Tokyo
1st August 2022

www.ingramcontent.com/pod-product-compliance
Ingram Content Group UK Ltd.
Pitfield, Milton Keynes, MK11 3LW, UK
UKHW040105210726
13892UKWH00005B/458